ESCAPES

ALSO BY JOY WILLIAMS

Novels
State of Grace
The Changeling
Breaking and Entering

Short Stories
Taking Care

Nonfiction
The Florida Keys: A History and Guide

ESCAPES

Stories

JOY WILLIAMS

THE ATLANTIC MONTHLY PRESS
NEW YORK

ACKNOWLEDGMENTS

I am grateful to the following publications, in which these stories originally appeared: *Esquire*: "The Skater," "The Blue Men" and "The Last Generation"; *Granta*: "The Little Winter"; *Grand Street*: "Rot," "Gurdjieff in the Sunshine State" and "Lu-Lu"; *The Chicago Tribune*: "Escapes"; *The Cornell Review*: "Bromeliads"; *Antaeus*: "White"; *The Antioch Review*: "The Route"; *Tendril*: "Health"; "Bromeliads," "The Skater," "Health" and "The Blue Men" were also printed in *The Best American Short Stories* (1978, 1985, 1986 and 1987); "Rot" also appeared in *Prize Stories 1988: The O. Henry Awards*.

The author gratefully acknowledges a grant from the National Endowment for the Arts that enabled her to complete this book.

Library of Congress Cataloging-in-Publication Data

Williams, Joy.
    Escapes: stories/Joy Williams
    Contents: Escapes—Rot—The skater—Lu-Lu—Gurdjieff in the
  Sunshine State—Bromeliads—The little winter—The route—
  Health—White—The blue men—The last generation
    ISBN 0-87113-332-6
    I. Title
    PS3573.I4496E8   1990   813'.54—dc20   89-14967

DESIGN BY LAURA HOUGH

The Atlantic Monthly Press
19 Union Square West
New York, NY 10003

FIRST PRINTING

CONTENTS

ESCAPES
1

ROT
15

THE SKATER
33

LU-LU
47

GURDJIEFF IN THE SUNSHINE STATE
57

Contents

BROMELIADS
63

THE LITTLE WINTER
73

THE ROUTE
97

HEALTH
111

WHITE
123

THE BLUE MEN
137

THE LAST GENERATION
151

ESCAPES

ESCAPES

WHEN I WAS VERY SMALL, MY FATHER SAID, "LIZZIE, I want to tell you something about your grandfather. Just before he died, he was alive. Fifteen minutes before."

I had never known my grandfather. This was the most extraordinary thing I had ever heard about him.

Still, I said, No.

"No!" my father said. "What do you mean, 'No.'" He laughed.

I shook my head.

"All right," my father said, "it was one minute before. I thought you were too little to know such things, but I see you're not. It was even less than a minute. It was one *moment* before."

"Oh stop teasing her," my mother said to my father.

"He's just teasing you, Lizzie," my mother said.

In warm weather once we drove up into the mountains, my mother, my father and I, and stayed for several days at a resort lodge on a lake. In the afternoons, horse races took place in the lodge. The horses were blocks of wood with numbers painted on them, moved from one end of the room to the other by ladies in ball gowns. There was a long pier that led out into the lake and at the end of the pier was a nightclub that had a twenty-foot-tall champagne glass on the roof. At night, someone would pull a switch and neon bubbles would spring out from the lit glass into the black air. I very much wanted such a glass on the roof of our own house and I wanted to be the one who, every night, would turn on the switch. My mother always said about this, "We'll see."

I saw an odd thing once, there in the mountains. I saw my father, pretending to be lame. This was in the midst of strangers in the gift shop of the lodge. The shop sold hand-carved canes, among many other things, and when I came in to buy bubble gum in the shape of cigarettes, to which I was devoted, I saw my father, hobbling painfully down the aisle, leaning heavily on a dully gleaming yellow cane, his shoulders hunched, one leg turned out at a curious angle. My handsome, healthy father, his face drawn in dreams. He looked at me. And then he looked away as though he did not know me.

My mother was a drinker. Because my father left us, I assumed he was not a drinker, but this may not have been the case. My mother loved me and was always kind to me. We spent a great deal of time together, my mother and I. This was before I knew how to read. I suspected there was a trick to reading, but I did not know the trick. Written words were something between me and a place I could not go. My mother went back and forth to that place all the time, but couldn't explain to me exactly what it was like there, I imagined it to be a different place.

As a very young child, my mother had seen the magician Houdini. Houdini had made an elephant disappear. He had also made an orange tree grow from a seed right on the stage. Bright oranges hung from the tree and he had picked them and thrown them out into the audience. People could eat the oranges or take them home, whatever they wanted.

How did he make the elephant disappear, I asked.

"He disappeared in a puff of smoke," my mother said. "Houdini said that even the elephant didn't know how it was done."

Was it a baby elephant, I asked.

My mother sipped her drink. She said that Houdini was more than a magician, he was an escape artist. She said that he could escape from handcuffs and chains and ropes.

"They put him in straitjackets and locked him in trunks and threw him in swimming pools and rivers and oceans and he escaped," my mother said. "He escaped from water-filled vaults. He escaped from coffins."

I said that I wanted to see Houdini.

"Oh, Houdini's dead, Lizzie," my mother said. "He died a long time ago. A man punched him in the stomach three times and he died."

Dead. I asked if he couldn't get out of being dead.

"He met his match there," my mother said.

She said that he turned a bowl of flowers into a pony who cantered around the stage.

"He sawed a lady in half too, Lizzie." Oh, how I wanted to be that lady, sawed in half and then made whole again!

My mother spoke happily, laughing. We sat at the kitchen

table and my mother was drinking from a small glass which rested snugly in her hand. It was my favorite glass too but she never let me drink from it. There were all kinds of glasses in our cupboard but this was the one we both liked. This was in Maine. Outside, in the yard, was our car which was an old blue convertible.

Was there blood, I asked.

"No, Lizzie, no. He was a magician!"

Did she cry, that lady, I wanted to know.

"I don't think so," my mother said. "Maybe he hypnotized her first."

It was winter. My father had never ridden in the blue convertible which my mother had bought after he had gone. The car was old then, and was rusted here and there. Beneath the rubber mat on my side, the passenger side, part of the floor had rusted through completely. When we went anywhere in the car, I would sometimes lift up the mat so I could see the road rushing past beneath us and feel the cold round air as it came up through the hole. I would pretend that the coldness was trying to speak to me, in the same way that words written down tried to speak. The air wanted to tell me something, but I didn't care about it, that's what I thought. Outside, the car stood in the snow.

I had a dream about the car. My mother and I were alone together as we always were, linked in our hopeless and uncomprehending love of one another, and we were driving to a house. It seemed to be our destination but we only arrived to move on. We drove again, always returning to the house which we would circle and leave, only to arrive at it again. As we drove, the inside of the car grew hair. The hair was gray and it grew and grew. I never told my mother about this dream just as I had never told her about my father leaning on the cane. I was a secretive person. In that way, I was like my mother.

4

I wanted to know more about Houdini. Was Houdini in love, did Houdini love someone, I asked.

"Rosabelle," my mother said. "He loved his wife, Rosabelle."

I went and got a glass and poured some ginger ale in it and I sipped my ginger ale slowly in the way that I had seen my mother sip her drink many, many times. Even then, I had the gestures down. I sat opposite her, very still and quiet, pretending.

But then I wanted to know was there magic in the way he loved her. Could he make her disappear. Could he make both of them disappear was the way I put my question.

"Rosabelle," my mother said. "No one knew anything about Rosabelle except that Houdini loved her. He never turned their love into loneliness which would have been beneath him of course."

We ate our supper and after supper my mother would have another little bit to drink. Then she would read articles from the newspaper aloud to me.

"My goodness," she said, "what a strange story. A hunter shot a bear who was carrying a woman's pocketbook in its mouth."

Oh, oh, I cried. I looked at the newspaper and struck it with my fingers. My mother read on, a little oblivious to me. The woman had lost her purse years before on a camping trip. Everything was still inside it, her wallet and her compact and her keys.

Oh, I cried. I thought this was terrible. I was frightened, thinking of my mother's pocketbook, the way she carried it always, and the poor bear too.

Why did the bear want to carry a pocketbook, I asked.

My mother looked up from the words in the newspaper. It was as though she had come back into the room I was in.

"Why, Lizzie," she said.

The poor bear, I said.

"Oh, the bear is all right," my mother said. "The bear got away."

I did not believe this was the case. She herself said the bear had been shot.

"The bear escaped," my mother said. "It says so right here," and she ran her finger along a line of words. "It ran back into the woods to its home." She stood up and came around the table and kissed me. She smelled then like the glass that was always in the sink in the morning, and the smell reminds me still of daring and deception, hopes and little lies.

I shut my eyes and in that way I felt I could not hear my mother. I saw the bear holding the pocketbook, walking through the woods with it, feeling fine in a different way and pretty too, then stopping to find something in it, wanting something, moving its big paw through the pocketbook's small things.

"Lizzie," my mother called to me. My mother did not know where I was which alarmed me. I opened my eyes.

"Don't cry, Lizzie," my mother said. She looked as though she were about to cry too. This was the way it often was at night, late in the kitchen, with my mother.

My mother returned to the newspaper and began to turn the pages. She called my attention to the drawing of a man holding a hat with stars sprinkling out of it. It was an advertisement for a magician who would be performing not far away. We decided we would see him. My mother knew just the seats she wanted for us, good seats, on the aisle close to the stage. We might be called up on the stage, she said, to be part of the performance. Magicians often used people from the audience, particularly children. I might even be given a rabbit.

I wanted a rabbit.

I put my hands on the table and I could see the rabbit between them. He was solid white in the front and solid black in the back as though he were made up of two rabbits. There are rabbits like that. I saw him there, before me on the table, a nice rabbit.

My mother went to the phone and ordered two tickets, and not many days after that, we were in our car driving to Portland for the matinee performance. I very much liked the word matinee. Matinee, matinee, I said. There was a broad hump on the floor between our seats and it was here where my mother put her little glass, the glass often full, never, it seemed, more than half empty. We chatted together and I thought we must have appeared interesting to others as we passed by in our convertible in winter. My mother spoke about happiness. She told me that the happiness that comes out of nowhere, out of nothing, is the very best kind. We paid no attention to the coldness which was speaking in the way that it had, but enjoyed the sun which beat through the windshield upon our pale hands.

My mother said that Houdini had black eyes and that white doves flew from his fingertips. She said that he escaped from a block of ice.

Did he look like my father, Houdini, I asked. Did he have a mustache.

"Your father didn't have a mustache," my mother said, laughing. "Oh, I wish I could be more like you."

Later, she said, "Maybe he didn't escape from a block of ice, I'm not sure about that. Maybe he wanted to, but he never did."

We stopped for lunch somewhere, a dark little restaurant along the road. My mother had cocktails and I myself drank something cold and sweet. The restaurant was not very nice. It smelled of smoke and dampness as though once it had burned

7

down, and it was so noisy that I could not hear my mother very well. My mother looked like a woman in a bar, pretty and disturbed, hunched forward saying, who do you think I look like, will you remember me? She was saying all matter of things. We lingered there, and then my mother asked the time of someone and seemed surprised. My mother was always surprised by time. Outside, there were woods of green fir trees whose lowest branches swept the ground, and as we were getting back into the car, I believed I saw something moving far back in the darkness of the woods beyond the slick, snowy square of the parking lot. It was the bear, I thought. Hurry, hurry, I thought. The hunter is playing with his children. He is making them something to play in as my father had once made a small playhouse for me. He is not the hunter yet. But in my heart I knew the bear was gone and the shape was just the shadow of something else in the afternoon.

My mother drove very fast but the performance had already begun when we arrived. My mother's face was damp and her good blouse had a spot on it. She went into the ladies' room and when she returned the spot was larger, but it was water now and not what it had been before. The usher assured us that we had not missed much. The usher said that the magician was not very good, that he talked and talked, he told a lot of jokes and then when you were bored and distracted, something would happen, something would have changed. The usher smiled at my mother. He seemed to like her, even know her in some way. He was a small man, like an old boy, balding. I did not care for him. He led us to our seats, but there were people sitting in them and there was a small disturbance as the strangers rearranged themselves. We were both expectant, my mother and I, and we watched the magician intently. My mother's lips were parted, and her eyes were bright. On the stage were a group of children about my age, each with a hand on a small cage the magician was holding. In the cage was a tiny bird. The magician would ask the children to jostle the cage occasionally and the bird would flutter against the bars so that everyone would see it was a real thing with bones and breath and feelings too. Each child announced that they had a firm grip on the bars. Then the magician put a cloth over the cage, gave a quick tug and cage and bird vanished. I was not surprised. It seemed just the kind of thing that was going to happen. I decided to withhold my applause when I saw that my mother's hands too were in her lap. There were several more tricks of the magician's invention, certainly nothing I would have asked him to do. Large constructions of many parts and colors were wheeled onto the stage. There were doors everywhere which the magician opened and slammed shut. Things came and went, all to the accompaniment of loud music. I was confused and grew hot. My mother too moved restlessly in the next seat. Then there was an intermission and we returned to the lobby.

"This man is a far, far cry from the great Houdini," my mother said.

What were his intentions exactly, I asked.

He had taken a watch from a man in the audience and smashed it for all to see with a hammer. Then the watch, unharmed, had reappeared behind the man's ear.

"A happy memory can be a very misleading thing," my mother said. "Would you like to go home?"

I did not want to leave really. I wanted to see it through. I held the glossy program in my hand and turned the pages. I stared hard at the print beneath the pictures and imagined all sorts of promises being made.

"Yes, we want to see how it's done, don't we, you and I," my mother said. "We want to get to the bottom of it."

I guessed we did.

"All right, Lizzie," my mother said, "but I have to get something out of the car. I'll be right back."

I waited for her in a corner of the lobby. Some children looked at me and I looked back. I had a package of gum cigarettes in my pocket and I extracted one carefully and placed the end in my mouth. I held the elbow of my right arm with my left hand and smoked the cigarette for a long time and then I folded it up in my mouth and I chewed it for a while. My mother had not yet returned when the performance began again. She was having a little drink, I knew, and she was where she went when she drank without me, somewhere in herself. It was not the place where words could take you but another place even. I stood alone in the lobby for a while, looking out into the street. On the sidewalk outside the theater, sand had been scattered and the sand ate through the ice in ugly holes. I saw no one like my mother who passed by. She was wearing a red coat. Once she had said to me, You've fallen out of love with me, haven't you, and I knew she was thinking I was someone else, but this had happened only once.

I heard the music from the stage and I finally returned to our seats. There were not as many people in the audience as before. On stage with the magician was a woman in a bathing suit and high-heeled shoes holding a chain saw. The magician demonstrated that the saw was real by cutting up several pieces of wood with it. There was the smell of torn wood for everyone to smell and sawdust on the floor for all to see. Then a table was wheeled out and the lady lay down on it in her bathing suit which was in two pieces. Her stomach was very white. The magician talked and waved the saw around. I suspected he was planning to cut the woman in half and I was eager to see this. I hadn't the slightest fear about this at all. I did wonder if he would be able to put her together again or if he would cut her in half only. The magician said that what was about to happen was too dreadful to be seen directly, that he did not want anyone to faint from the sight, so he brought out a small screen and placed it in front of the lady so that we could no longer see her white stomach, although everyone could still see her face and her shoes. The screen seemed unnecessary to me and I would have preferred to have been seated on the other side of it. Several people in the audience screamed. The lady who was about to be sawed in half began to chew on her lip and her face looked worried.

It was then that my mother appeared on the stage. She was crouched over a little, for she didn't have her balance back from having climbed up there. She looked large and strange in her red coat. The coat, which I knew very well, seemed the strangest thing. Someone screamed again, but more uncertainly. My mother moved toward the magician, smiling and speaking and gesturing with her hands, and the magician said, No, I can't of course, you should know better than this, this is a performance, you can't just appear like this, please sit down . . .

My mother said, But you don't understand I'm willing, though I know the hazards and it's not that I believe you, no one would believe you for a moment but you can trust me, that's right, your faith in me would be perfectly placed because I'm not part of this, that's why I can be trusted because I don't know how it's done . . .

Someone near me said, Is she kidding, that woman, what's her plan, she comes out of nowhere and wants to be cut in half . . .

Lady . . . the magician said, and I thought a dog might appear for I knew a dog named Lady who had a collection of colored balls.

My mother said, Most of us don't understand I know and it's just as well because the things we understand that's it for them, that's just the way we are . . .

She probably thought she was still in that place in herself, but everything she said were the words coming from her mouth. Her lipstick was gone. Did she think she was in disguise, I wondered.

But why not, my mother said, to go and come back, that's what we want, that's why we're here and why can't we expect something to be done you can't expect us every day we get tired of showing up every day you can't get away with this forever then it was different but you should be thinking about the children . . . She moved a little in a crooked fashion, speaking.

My God, said a voice, that woman's drunk. Sit down, please! someone said loudly.

My mother started to cry then and she stumbled and pushed her arms out before her as though she were pushing away someone who was trying to hold her, but no one was trying to hold her. The orchestra began to play and people began to clap. The usher ran out onto the stage and took my mother's hand. All this happened in an instant. He said something to her, he held her hand and she did not resist his holding it, then slowly the two of them moved down the few steps that led to the stage and up the aisle until they stopped beside me for the usher knew I was my mother's child. I followed them, of course, although in my mind I continued to sit in my seat. Everyone watched us leave. They did not notice that I remained there among them, watching too.

We went directly out of the theater and into the streets, my mother weeping on the little usher's arm. The shoulders of his jacket were of cardboard and there was gold braid looped around it. We were being taken away to be murdered which seemed reasonable to me. The usher's ears were large and he had a bump on his neck above the collar of his shirt. As we walked he said little soft things to my mother which gradually seemed to be comforting her. I hated him. It was not easy to walk together along the frozen sidewalks of the city. There was a belt on my mother's coat and I hung onto that as we moved unevenly along.

Look, I've pulled myself through, he said. You can pull yourself through. He was speaking to my mother.

We went into a coffee shop and sat down in a booth. You can collect yourself in here, he said. You can sit here as long as you want and drink coffee and no one will make you leave. He asked me if I wanted a donut. I would not speak to him. If he addressed me again, I thought, I would bite him. On the wall over the counter were pictures of sandwiches and pies. I did not want to be there and I did not take off either my mittens or my coat. The little usher went up to the counter and brought back coffee for my mother and a donut on a plate for me. Oh, my mother said, what have I done, and she swung her head from side to side.

I could tell right away about you, the usher said. You've got to pull yourself together. It took jumping off a bridge for me and breaking both legs before I got turned around. You don't want to let it go that far.

My mother looked at him. I can't imagine, my mother said.

Outside, a child passed by, walking with her sled. She looked behind her often and you could tell she was admiring the way the sled followed her so quickly on its runners.

You're a mother, the usher said to my mother, you've got to pull yourself through.

His kindness made me feel he had tied us up with rope. At

last he left us and my mother laid her head down upon the table and fell asleep. I had never seen my mother sleeping and I watched her as she must once have watched me, the same way everyone watches a sleeping thing, not knowing how it would turn out or when. Then slowly I began to eat the donut with my mittened hands. The sour hair of the wool mingled with the tasteless crumbs and this utterly absorbed my attention. I pretended someone was feeding me.

As it happened, my mother was not able to pull herself through, but this was later. At the time, it was not so near the end and when my mother woke we found the car and left Portland, my mother saying my name. Lizzie, she said. Lizzie. I felt as though I must be with her somewhere and that she knew that too, but not in that old blue convertible traveling home in the dark, the soft, stained roof ballooning up in the way I knew it looked from the outside. I got out of it, but it took me years.

ROT

LUCY WAS WATCHING THE STREET WHEN AN OLD
Ford Thunderbird turned into their driveway. She had never
seen the car before and her husband, Dwight, was driving it.
One of Dwight's old girlfriends leapt from the passenger seat
and ran toward the house. Her name was Caroline, she had
curly hair and big white teeth, more than seemed normal, and
Lucy liked her the least of all of Dwight's old girlfriends. Nevertheless, when she came inside, Lucy said, "Would you like a glass
of water or something?"

"I was the horn," Caroline said. "That car doesn't have
one so I was it. I'd yell out the window, 'Watch out!'"

"Were you the brakes too or just the horn?" Lucy asked.

"It has brakes," Caroline said, showing her startling teeth.
She went into the living room and said, "Hello, rug." She always
spoke to the rug lying there. The rug was from Mexico with

15

birds of different colors flying across it. All of the birds had long, white eyes. Dwight and Caroline had brought the rug back from the Yucatán when they had gone snorkeling there years before. Some of the coves were so popular that the fish could scarcely be seen for all the suntan oil floating in the water. At Garrafon in Isla Mujeres, Dwight told Lucy, he had raised his head and seen a hundred people bobbing facedown over the rocks of the reef and a clean white tampon bobbing there among them. Caroline had said at the time, "It's disgusting, but it's obviously some joke."

Caroline muttered little things to the rug, showing off, Lucy thought, although she wasn't speaking Spanish to it, she didn't know Spanish. Lucy looked out the window at Dwight sitting in the Thunderbird. It was old with new paint, black, with a white top and portholes and skirts. He looked a little big for it. He got out abruptly and ran to the house as though through rain, but there was no rain. It was a gray, still day in spring, just before Easter, with an odious weight to the air. Recently, when they had been coming inside, synthetic stuff from Easter baskets had been traveling in with them, the fake nesting matter, the pastel and crinkly stuff of Easter baskets. Lucy couldn't imagine where they kept picking it up from, but no festive detritus came in this time.

Dwight gave her a hard, wandering kiss on the mouth. Lately, it was as though he were trying out kisses, trying to adjust them.

"You'll tell me all about this, I guess," Lucy said.

"Lucy," Dwight said solemnly.

Caroline joined them and said, "I've got to be off. I don't know the time, but I bet I can guess it to within a minute. I can do that," she assured Lucy. Caroline closed her eyes. Her teeth seemed still to be looking out at them, however. "Five ten," she said after a while. Lucy looked at the clock on the wall which showed ten minutes past five. She shrugged.

"That car is some cute," Caroline said, giving Dwight a little squeeze. "Isn't it some cute?" she said to Lucy. "Your Dwight's been tracking this car for days."

"I bought it from the next of kin," Dwight said.

Lucy looked at him impassively. She was not a girl who was quick to alarm.

"I was down at the Aquarium last week looking at the fish," Dwight began.

"Oh, that Aquarium," Lucy said.

The Aquarium was where a baby seal had been put to sleep because he was born too ugly to be viewed by children. He had not been considered viewable so off he went. The Aquarium offended Lucy. "I like fish," Dwight had told Lucy when she asked why he spent so much of his free time at the Aquarium. "Men like fish."

"And when I came out into the parking lot, next to our car was this little Thunderbird and there was a dead man sitting behind the wheel."

"Isn't that something!" Caroline exclaimed.

"I was the first to find him," Dwight said. "I'm no expert but that man was gone."

"What did this dead man look like?" Lucy asked Dwight.

He thought for a moment, then said, "He looked like someone in the movies. He had a large head."

"He didn't resemble you, did he?" she asked.

"Oh no, darling, not in the slightest."

"In any case," Lucy said a little impatiently.

"In any case," Dwight said, "this car just jumped at me, you know the way some things do. I knew I just had to have this car, it was just so pretty. It's the same age as you are, darling. That was the year the good things came out."

Lucy made a face for she wearied of references to her youth. She was almost twenty-five years younger than Dwight. Actually, theirs was rather a peculiar story.

"This car is almost cherry," Dwight said, gesturing out at it, "and now it's ours."

"That car is not almost cherry," Lucy said. "A man died in it. I would say that this car was about as un-cherry as you can get." She went on vehemently in this way for awhile.

Caroline gazed at her, her lips parted, her teeth making no judgment. Then she said, "I've got to get back to my lonely home." She did not live far away. Almost everybody they knew, and a lot of people they didn't, lived close by. "Now you two have fun in that car, it's a sweet little car." She kissed Dwight and he patted her back in an avuncular fashion as he walked her to the door. The air outside had a faint, thin smell of fruit and rubber. A siren screamed through it.

When Dwight returned, Lucy said, "I don't want a car a man died in for my birthday."

"It's not your birthday coming up, is it?"

Lucy admitted it was not, although Dwight often planned for her birthday months in advance. She blushed.

"It's funny how some people live longer than others, isn't it," she finally said.

❧

Lucy and Dwight had been married for five years. When Dwight had first seen her, he was twenty-five years old and she was a four-month-old baby.

"I'm gonna marry you," Dwight said to the baby. People heard him. He was tall and had black hair, and was wearing a leather jacket that a girlfriend had sewed a violet silk liner into. It was a New Year's Eve party at this girlfriend's house and the girl was standing beside him. "Oh, right," she said. She didn't see anything particularly intriguing about this baby. They could make better babies than this, she thought. Lucy lay in a white wicker basket on a sofa. Her hair was sparse and her expression solemn. "You're gonna be my wife," Dwight said. He was very good with babies and good with children too. When Lucy was five, her favorite things were pop-up books in which one found what was missing by pushing or pulling or turning a tab, and for her birthday Dwight bought her fifteen of these, surely as many as had ever been produced. When she was ten he bought her a playhouse and filled it with balloons. Dwight was good with adolescents as well. When she was fourteen, he rented her a horse for a year. As for women, he had a special touch with them, as all his girlfriends would attest. Dwight wasn't faithful to Lucy as she was growing up, but he was attentive and devoted. Dwight kept up the pace nicely. And all the time Lucy was stoically growing up, learning how to dress herself and read, letting her hair grow, then cutting it all off, joining clubs and playing records, doing her algebra, going on dates, Dwight was out in the world. He always sent her little stones from the places he visited and she ordered them by size or color and put them in and out of boxes and jars until there came to be so many she grew confused as to where each had come from. This alarmed her at first, and then it annoyed her. At about the time Lucy didn't care if she saw another little stone in her life, they got married. They bought a house and settled in. The house was a large, comfortable one, large enough, was the inference, to accommodate growth of various sorts. Things were all right.

Dwight was like a big strange book where Lucy just needed to turn the pages and there everything was already.

❧

They went out and looked at the Thunderbird in the waning light.

"It's a beauty, isn't it," Dwight said. "Wide whites, complete engine dress." He opened the hood, exposing the gleaming motor. Dwight was happy, his inky eyes shone. When he slammed the hood shut there was a soft rattling as of pebbles being thrown.

"What's that?" Lucy asked.

"What's what, my sweet?"

"That," Lucy said, "on the ground." She picked up a piece of rust, as big as her small hand and very light. Dwight peered at it. As she was trying to hand it to him, it dropped and crumbled.

"It looked so solid, I didn't check underneath," Dwight said. "I'll have some body men come over tomorrow and look at it. I'm sure it's no problem, just superficial stuff."

She ran her fingers behind the rocker panel of the door and came up with a handful of flakes.

"I don't know why you'd want to make it worse," Dwight said.

The next morning, two men were scooting around on their backs beneath the T-Bird, poking here and there with screwdrivers and squinting at the undercarriage. Lucy, who enjoyed a leisurely breakfast, was still in the kitchen, finishing it. As she ate her cereal, she studied the milk carton, a panel of which made a request for organs. Lucy was aware of a new determination in the world to keep things going. She rinsed her bowl and went outside just as the two men had slipped from beneath the car and were standing up, staring at Dwight. Gouts and clots of rust littered the drive.

"This for your daughter here?" one of them said.

"No," Dwight said irritably.

"I wouldn't give this to my daughter."

"It's not for anyone like that!" Dwight said.

"Bottom's just about to go," the other one said. "Riding along, these plates give, floor falls out, your butt's on the road. You need new pans at least. Pans are no problem." He chewed on his thumbnail. "It's rusted out too where the leaf springs meet the frame. Needs some work, no doubt about that. Somebody's done a lot of work but it needs a lot more work for sure. Donny, get me the Hemmings out of the truck."

The other man ambled off and returned with a thick brown catalogue.

"Maybe you should trade up," the first man said. "Get a car with a solid frame."

Dwight shook his head. "You can't repair it?"

"Why sure we can repair it!" Donny said. "You can get everything for these cars, all the parts, you got yourself a classic here!" He thumbed through the catalogue until he came to a page which offered the services of something called *The T-Bird Sanctuary*. The Sanctuary seemed to be a wrecking yard. A grainy photograph showed a jumble of cannibalized cars scattered among trees. It was the kind of picture that looked as though it had been taken furtively with a concealed camera.

"I'd trade up," the other man said. "Lookit over here, this page here, *Fifty-seven F-Bird supercharged, torch red, total body-off restoration, nothing left undone, ready to show . . .*"

"Be still, my heart," Donny said.

"You know if you are going to stick with this car you got,"

the other man said, "and I'm not advising you to, you should paint it the original color. This black ain't original." He opened the door and pointed at a smudge near the hinges. "See here, Powderblue."

"Starmist blue," Donny said, looking at him furiously.

The men glared at each other and when it appeared that they were about to come to blows, Lucy returned to the house. She stood inside, thinking, looking out at the street. When she had been a little girl on her way to school, she had once found an envelope on the street with her name on it, but there hadn't been anything in the envelope.

"We're getting another opinion," Dwight said when he came in. "We're taking it over to Boris, the best in the business."

They drove to the edge of town, to where another town began, to a big brown building there. Lucy enjoyed the car. It handled very well, she thought. They hurtled along, even though bigger cars passed them.

Boris was small, bald and stern. The German shepherd that stood beside him seemed remarkably large. His paws were delicately rounded but each was the size of a football. There was room, easily, for another German shepherd inside him, Lucy thought. Boris drove the Thunderbird onto a lift and elevated it. He walked slowly beneath it, his hands on his hips. Not a hair grew from his head. He lowered the car down and said, "Hopeless." When neither Lucy nor Dwight spoke, he shouted, "Worthless. Useless." The German shepherd sighed as though he had heard this prognosis many times.

"What about where the leaf springs meet the frame?" Lucy said. The phrase enchanted her.

Boris moved his hands around and then clutched and twisted them together in a pleading fashion.

Rot

"How can I make you nice people understand that it is hopeless? What can I say so that you will hear me, so that you will believe me? Do you like ripping up one-hundred-dollar bills? Is this what you want to do with the rest of your life? What kind of masochists are you? It would be wicked of me to give you hope. This car is unrestorable. It is full of rust and rot. Rust is a living thing, it breathes, it eats and it is swallowing up your car. These quarters and rockers have already been replaced, once, twice, who knows how many times. You will replace them again. It is nothing to replace quarters and rockers! How can I save you from your innocence and foolishness and delusions. You take out a bad part, say, you solder in new metal, you line-weld it tight, you replace the whole rear end, say, and what have you accomplished, you have accomplished only a small part of what is necessary, you have accomplished hardly anything! I can see you feel dread and nausea at what I'm saying but it is nothing compared to the dread and nausea you will feel if you continue in this unfortunate project. Stop wasting your thoughts! Rot like this cannot be stayed. This brings us to the question, What is man? with its three subdivisions, What can he know? What ought he do? What may he hope? Questions which concern us all, even you, little lady."

"What!" Dwight said.

"My suggestion is to drive this car," Boris said in a calmer tone, "enjoy it, but for the spring and summer only, then dump it, part it out. Otherwise, you'll be putting in new welds, more and more new welds, but always the collapse will be just ahead of you. Years will pass and then will come the day when there is nothing to weld the weld to, there is no frame, nothing. Once rot, then nothing." He bowed, then retired to his office, which was sheeted with one-way glass.

Driving home, Dwight said, "You never used to hear about rust and rot all the time. It's new, this rust and rot business. You don't know what's around you any more."

Lucy knew Dwight was depressed and tried to look concerned, though in truth she didn't care much about the T-Bird. She was distracted by a tune that was going through her head. It was a song she remembered hearing when she was a little baby, about a tiny ant being at his doorway. She finally told Dwight about it and hummed the tune.

"Do you remember that little song?" she asked.

"Almost," Dwight said.

"What was that about anyway," Lucy asked. "The tiny ant didn't do anything, he was just waiting at his doorway."

"It was just nonsense stuff you'd sing to a little baby," Dwight said. He looked at her vaguely and said, "My sweet . . ."

Lucy called up her friend Daisy and told her about the black Thunderbird. She did not mention rot. Daisy was ten years older than Lucy and was one of the last of Dwight's girlfriends. Daisy had recently had one of her legs amputated. There had been a climbing accident and then she had just let things go on for too long. She was a tall, boyish-looking woman who before the amputation had always worn jeans. Now she slung herself about in skirts, for she found it disturbed people less when she wore a skirt, but when she went to the beach she wore a bathing suit, and she didn't care if she disturbed people or not because she loved the beach, the water, so still and so heavy, hiding so much.

"I didn't read in the paper about a dead man just sitting

in his car like that," Daisy said. "Don't they usually report such things? It's unusual, isn't it?"

Lucy had fostered Daisy's friendship because she knew Daisy was still in love with Dwight. If someone, God, for example, had asked Daisy if she'd rather have her leg back or Dwight, she would have said, "Dwight." Lucy felt excited about this and at the same time mystified and pitying. Knowing it always cheered Lucy up when she felt out of sorts.

"Did I tell you about the man in the supermarket with only one leg?" Daisy asked. "I had never seen him before. He was with his wife and baby and instead of being in the mother's arms the baby was in a stroller so the three of them took up a great deal of room in the aisle, and when I turned down the aisle I became entangled with this little family. I felt that I had known this man all my life, of course. People were smiling at us. Even the wife was smiling. It was dreadful."

"You should find someone," Lucy said without much interest.

Daisy's leg was in ashes in a drawer in a church garden, waiting for the rest of her.

"Oh no, no," Daisy said modestly. "So!" she said, "You're going to have another car!"

It was almost suppertime and there was the smell of meat on the air. Two small, brown birds hopped across the patchy grass and Lucy watched them with interest for birds seldom frequented their neighborhood. Whenever there were more than three birds in a given place, it was considered an infestation and a variety of measures were taken which reduced their numbers to an acceptable level. Lucy remembered that when she was little, the birds that flew overhead sometimes cast shadows on the ground. There were flocks of them at times and she remembered hearing the creaking of their wings, but she supposed that was just the sort of thing a child might remember, having seen or heard it only once.

She set the dining-room table for three as this was the night each spring when Rosette would come for dinner, bringing shad and shad roe, Dwight's favorite meal. Rosette had been the most elegant of Dwight's girlfriends, and the one with the smallest waist. She was now married to a man named Bob. When Rosette had been Dwight's girlfriend, she had been called Muffin. For the last five springs, ever since Lucy and Dwight had been married, she would have the shad flown down from the North and she would bring it to their house and cook it. Yet even though shad was his favorite fish and he only got it once a year, Dwight would be coming home a little late this night because he was getting another opinion on the T-Bird. Lucy no longer accompanied him on these discouraging expeditions.

Rosette appeared in a scant, white cocktail dress and red high-heeled shoes. She had brought her own china, silver, candles and wine. She reset the table, dimmed the lights and made Lucy and herself large martinis. They sat, waiting for Dwight, speaking in an aimless way about things. Rosette and Bob were providing a foster home for two delinquents whose names were Jerry and Jackie.

"What awful children," Rosette said. "They're so homely too. They were cuter when they were younger, now their noses are really long and their jaws are odd-looking too. I gave them bunny baskets this year and Jackie wrote me a note saying that what she really needed was a prescription for birth-control pills."

When Dwight arrived, Rosette was saying, "Guilt's not a bad thing to have. There are worse things to have than guilt." She looked admiringly at Dwight and said, "You're a handsome eyeful." She made him a martini which he drank quickly, then she made them all another one. Drinking hers, Lucy stood and watched the T-Bird in the driveway. It was a dainty car, and the paint was so black it looked wet. Rosette prepared the fish with great solemnity, bending over Lucy's somewhat dirty broiler. They all ate in a measured way. Lucy tried to eat the roe one small egg at a time but found that this was impossible.

"I saw Jerry this afternoon walking down the street carrying a Weedwacker," Dwight said. "Does he do yard work now? Yard work's a good occupation for a boy."

"Delinquents aren't always culprits," Rosette said. "That's what many people don't understand, but no, Jerry is not doing yard work, he probably stole that thing off someone's lawn. Bob tries to talk to him but Jerry doesn't heed a word he says. Bob's not very convincing."

"How is Bob?" Lucy asked.

"Husband Bob is a call I never should have answered," Rosette said.

Lucy crossed her arms over her stomach and squeezed herself with delight because Rosette said the same thing each year when she was asked about Bob.

"Life with Husband Bob is a long twilight of drinking and listless anecdote," Rosette said.

Lucy giggled, because Rosette always said this, too.

The next day, Dwight told Lucy of his intentions to bring the T-Bird into the house. "She won't last long on the street,"

he said. "She's a honey but she's tired. Elements are hard on a car and it's the elements that have done this sweet little car in. We'll put her in the living room which is under-furnished anyway and it will be like living with a work of art right in our living room. We'll keep her shined up and sit inside her and talk. It's very peaceful inside that little car, you know."

The T-Bird looked alert and coquettish as they spoke around it.

"That car was meant to know the open road," Lucy said. "I think we should drive it till it drops." Dwight looked at her sorrowfully and she widened her eyes, not believing she had said such a thing. "Well," she said, "I don't think a car should be in a house, but maybe we could bring it in for a little while and then if we don't like it we could take it out again."

He put his arms around her and embraced her and she could hear his heart pounding away in his chest with gratitude and excitement.

Lucy called Daisy on the telephone. The banging and sawing had already begun. "Men go odd in different ways than women," Daisy said. "That's always been the case. For example, I read that men are exploring ways of turning the earth around toxic waste dumps into glass by the insertion of high-temperature electric probes. A woman would never think of something like that."

Dwight worked feverishly for days. He removed the picture window, took down the wall, shored up the floor, built a ramp, drained the car of all its fluids so it wouldn't leak on the rug, pushed it into the house, replaced the studs, put back the window, erected fresh Sheetrock and repainted the entire room. Lucy was amazed that it was so easy to tear a wall down and put it back up again. In the room, the car looked like a big doll's car. But it didn't look bad inside the house at all and Lucy didn't

28

mind it being there, although she didn't like it when Dwight raised the hood. She didn't care for the hood being raised one bit and always lowered it when she saw it was up. She thought about the Thunderbird most often at night when she was in bed lying beside Dwight and then she would marvel at its silent, unseen presence in the room beside them, taking up space, so strange and shining and full of rot.

They would sit frequently in the car, in their house, not going anywhere, looking through the windshield out at the window and through the window to the street. They didn't invite anyone over for this. Soon, Dwight took to sitting in the car by himself. Dwight was tired. It was taking him a while to bounce back from the carpentry. Lucy saw him there one day behind the wheel, one arm bent and dangling over the glossy door, his eyes shut, his mouth slightly open, his hair as black as she had ever seen it. She couldn't remember the first time she had noticed him, really noticed him, the way he must have first noticed her when she'd been a baby.

"I wish you'd stop that, Dwight," she said, "sitting there pale like that."

He opened his eyes. "You should try this by yourself," he said. "Just try it and tell me what you think."

She sat for some time in the car alone, then went into the kitchen where Dwight stood, drinking water. It was a gray day, with a gray careless light falling everywhere.

"I had the tiniest feeling in there that the point being made was that something has robbed this world of its promise," Lucy said. She did not have a sentimental nature.

Dwight was holding a glass of water in one of his large hands, frowning a little at it. Water poured into the sink and down the drain, part of the same water he was drinking. On the counter was a television set with a picture but no sound. Men were wheeling two stretchers out of a house and across a lawn and on each stretcher was a long still thing covered in a green cloth. The house was a cement-block house with two metal chairs on the porch with little cushions on them, and under the roof's overhang a basket of flowers swung.

"Is this the only channel we ever get?" Lucy said. She turned the water faucet off.

"It's the news, Lucy."

"I've seen this news a hundred times before. It's always this kind of news."

"This is the Sun Belt, Lucy."

The way he kept saying her name began to irritate her. "Well, Dwight," she said. "Dwight, Dwight, Dwight."

Dwight looked at her mildly and went back to the living room. Lucy trailed after him. They both looked at the car and Lucy said to it, "I'd like an emerald ring. I'd like a baby boy."

"You don't ask it for things, Lucy," Dwight said.

"I'd like a Porsche Carrera," Lucy said to it.

"Are you crazy or what!" Dwight demanded.

"I would like a little baby," she mused.

"You were a little baby once," Dwight said.

"Well, I know that."

"So isn't that enough?"

She looked at him uneasily, then said, "Do you know what I used to like that you did? You'd say, 'That's my wife's favorite color . . .' or 'That's just what my wife says . . .' " Dwight gazed at her from his big, inky eyes. "And of course your wife was me!" she exclaimed. "I always thought that was kind of sexy."

"We're not talking sex any more, Lucy," he said. She blushed.

Dwight got into the Thunderbird and rested his hands on

the wheel. She saw his fingers pressing against the horn rim which made no sound.

"I don't think this car should be in the house," Lucy said, still fiercely blushing.

"It's a place where I can think, Lucy."

"But it's in the middle of the living room! It takes up practically the whole living room!"

"A man's got to think, Lucy. A man's got to prepare for things."

"Where did you think before we got married," she said crossly.

"All over, Lucy. I thought of you everywhere. You were part of everything."

Lucy did not want to be part of everything. She did not want to be part of another woman's kissing, for example. She did not want to be part of Daisy's leg which she was certain, in their time, had played its part and been something Dwight had paid attention to. She did not want to be part of a great many things that she could mention.

"I don't want to be part of everything," she said.

"Life is different from when I was young and you were a little baby," Dwight said.

"I never did want to be part of everything," she said excitedly.

Dwight worked his shoulders back into the seat and stared out the window.

"Maybe the man who had this car before died of a broken heart, did you ever think of that?" Lucy said. When he said nothing, she said, "I don't want to start waiting on you again, Dwight." Her face had cooled off now.

"You wait the way you want to wait," Dwight said. "You've

got to know what you want while you're waiting." He patted the seat beside him and smiled at her. It wasn't just a question of moving this used-up thing out again, she knew that. Time wasn't moving sideways the way it had always seemed to her to move but was climbing upward, then falling back, then lurching in a circle like some poisoned, damaged thing. Eventually, she sat down next to him. She looked through the glass at the other glass, then past that.

"It's raining," Lucy said.

There was a light rain falling, a warm spring rain. As she watched, it fell more quickly. It was silverish, but as it fell faster it appeared less and less like rain and she could almost hear it rattling as it struck the street.

THE SKATER

ANNIE AND TOM AND MOLLY ARE LOOKING AT boarding schools. Molly is the applicant, fourteen years old. Annie and Tom are the mom and dad. This is how they are referred to by the admissions directors. "Now if Mom and Dad would just make themselves comfortable while we steal Molly away for a moment . . ." Molly is stolen away and Tom and Annie drink coffee. There are brown donuts on a plate. Colored slides are slapped upon a screen showing children earnestly learning and growing and caring through the seasons. These things have been captured. Rather, it's clear that's what they're getting at. The children's faces blur in Tom's mind. And all those autumn leaves. All those laboratories and playing fields and bell towers.

It is winter and there is snow on the ground. They have flown in from California and rented a car. Their plan is to see seven New England boarding schools in five days. Icicles hang from the admissions building. Tom gazes at them. They are lovely and refractive. They are formed and then they vanish. Tom looks away.

Annie is sitting on the other side of the room, puzzling over a mathematics problem. There are sheets of problems all over the waiting room. The sheets are to keep parents and kids on their toes as they wait. The cold, algebraic problems are presented in little stories. Five times as many girls as boys are taking music lessons or trees are growing at different rates or ladies in a bridge club are lying about their age. The characters and situations are invented only to be exiled to measurement. Watching Annie search for solutions makes Tom's heart ache. He remembers a class he took once himself, almost twenty years ago, a class in myth. In mythical stories, it seems, there were two ways to disaster. One of the ways was to answer an unanswerable question. The other was to fail to answer an answerable question.

Down a corridor there are several shut doors and behind one is Molly. Molly is their living child. Tom and Annie's other child, Martha, has been dead a year. Martha was one year older than Molly. Now Molly is her age. Martha choked to death in her room on a piece of bread. It was early in the morning and she was getting ready for school. The radio was playing and two disc jockeys called the Breakfast Flakes chattered away between songs.

The weather is bad, the roads are slippery. From the backseat, Molly says, "He asked what my favorite ice cream was and

I said, 'Quarterback Crunch.' Then he asked who was President of the United States when the school was founded and I said, 'No one.' Wasn't that good?"

"I hate trick questions," Annie says.

"Did you like the school?" Tom asks.

"Yeah," Molly says.

"What did you like best about it?"

"I liked the way our guide, you know, Peter, just walked right across the street that goes through the campus and the cars just stopped. You and Mom were kind of hanging back, looking both ways and all, but Peter and I just trucked right across."

Molly was chewing gum that smelled like oranges.

"Peter was cute," Molly says.

Tom and Annie and Molly sit around a small table in their motel room. Snow accumulates beyond the room's walls. Molly drinks cranberry juice from a box and Tom and Annie drink Scotch. They are nowhere. The brochure that the school sent them states that the school is located thirty-five miles from Boston. Nowhere! They are all exhausted and merely sit there, regarding their beverages. The television set is chained to the wall. This is indicative, Tom thinks, of considerable suspicion on the part of the management. There was also a four-dollar deposit on the room key. The management, when Tom checked in, was in the person of a child about Molly's age, a boy eating from a bag of potato chips and doing his homework.

"There's a kind of light that glows in the bottom of the water in an atomic reactor that exists nowhere else, do you know that?" the boy said to Tom.

"Is that right?" Tom said.

"Yeah," the boy said, and marked the book he was reading with his pencil. "I think that's right."

The motel room is darkly paneled and there is a picture of a moose between the two beds. The moose is knee-deep in a lake and he has raised his head to some sound, the sound of a hunter approaching, one would imagine. Water drips from his muzzle. The woods he gazes at are dark. Annie looks at the picture. The moose is preposterous and doomed. After a few moments, after she has finished her Scotch, Annie realizes she is waiting to hear the sound. She goes into the bathroom and washes her hands and face. The towel is thin. It smells as if it's been line-dried. It was her idea that Molly go away to school. She wants Molly to be free. She doesn't want her to be afraid. She fears that she is making her afraid, as she is afraid. Annie hears Molly and Tom talking in the other room and then she hears Molly laugh. She raises her fingers to the window frame and feels the cold air seeping in. She adjusts the lid to the toilet tank. It shifts slightly. She washes her hands again. She goes into the room and sits on one of the beds.

"What are you laughing about?" she says. She means to be offhand, but her words come out heavily.

"Did you see the size of that girl's radio in the dorm room we visited?" Molly says, laughing. "It was the biggest radio I'd ever seen. I told Daddy there was a real person lying in it, singing." Molly giggles. She pulls her turtleneck sweater up to just below her eyes.

Annie laughs, then she thinks she has laughed at something terrible, the idea of someone lying trapped and singing. She raises her hands to her mouth. She had not seen a radio large enough to hold anyone. She saw children in classes, in laboratories in some brightly painted basement. The children were dissecting sheep's eyes. "Every winter term in Biology you've got to dissect sheep's eyes," their guide said wearily. "The colors are really nice though." She saw sacks of laundry tumbled down a stairwell with names stenciled on them. Now she tries not to see a radio large enough to hold anyone singing.

At night, Tom drives in his dreams. He dreams of ice, of slick treachery. All night he fiercely holds the wheel and turns in the direction of the skid.

In the morning when he returns the key, the boy has been replaced by an old man with liver spots the size of quarters on his hands. Tom thinks of asking where the boy is, but then realizes he must be in school learning about eerie, deathly light. The bills the old man returns to Tom are soft as cloth.

In California, they live in a canyon. Martha's room is not situated with a glimpse of the ocean like some of the other rooms. It faces a rocky ledge where owls nest. The canyon is cold and full of small birds and bitter-smelling shrubs. The sun moves quickly through it. When the rocks are touched by the sun, they steam. All of Martha's things remain in her room—the radio, the posters and mirrors and books. It is a "guest" room now, although no one ever refers to it in that way. They refer to it as "Martha's room." But it has become a guest room, even though there are never any guests.

The rental car is blue and without distinction. It is a four-door sedan with automatic transmission and a poor turning circle. Martha would have been mortified by it. Martha had a boyfriend who, with his brothers, owned a monster truck. The Super Swamper tires were as tall as Martha, and all the driver of an ordinary car would see when it passed by was its colorful undercarriage with its huge shock and suspension coils, its long orange stabilizers. For hours on a Saturday they would wallow in sloughs and rumble and pitch across stony creek beds, and then they would wash and wax the truck or, as James, the boyfriend, would say, dazzle the hog. The truck's name was Bear. Tom and Annie didn't care for James, and they hated and feared Bear. Martha loved Bear. She wore a red and white peaked cap with MONSTER TRUCK stenciled on it. After Martha died, Molly put the cap on once or twice. She thought it would help her feel closer to Martha but it didn't. The sweatband smelled slightly of shampoo, but it was just a cap.

Tom pulls into the frozen field that is the parking lot for the Northwall School. The admissions office is very cold. The receptionist is wearing an old worn Chesterfield coat and a scarf. Someone is playing a hesitant and plaintive melody on a piano in one of the nearby rooms. They are shown the woodlot, the cafeteria, and the arts department, where people are hammering out their own silver bracelets. They are shown the language department, where a class is doing tarot card readings in French. They pass a room and hear a man's voice say, "Matter is a sort of blindness."

While Molly is being interviewed, Tom and Annie walk to the barn. The girls are beautiful in this school. The boys look a little dull. Two boys run past them, both wearing jeans and denim jackets. Their hair is short and their ears are red. They appear to be pretending that they are in a drama, that they are being filmed. They dart and feint. One stumbles into a building while the other crouches outside, tossing his head and scowling, throwing an imaginary knife from hand to hand.

Annie tries a door to the barn but it is latched from the inside. She walks around the barn in her high heels. The hem of her coat dangles. She wears gloves on her pale hands. Tom walks beside her, his own hands in his pockets. A flock of starlings fly overhead in an oddly tight formation. A hawk flies above them. The hawk will not fall upon them, clenched like this. If one would separate from the flock, then the hawk could fall.

"I don't know about this 'matter is a sort of blindness' place," Tom says. "It's not what I had in mind."

Annie laughs but she's not paying attention. She wants to get into the huge barn. She tugs at another door. Dirt smears the palms of her gloves. Then suddenly, the wanting leaves her face.

"Martha would like this school, wouldn't she," she says.

"We don't know, Annie," Tom says. "Please don't, Annie."

"I feel that I've lived my whole life in one corner of a room," Annie says. "That's the problem. It's just having always been in this one corner. And now I can't see anything. I don't even know the room, do you see what I'm saying?"

Tom nods but he doesn't see the room. The sadness in him has become his blood, his life flowing in him. There's no room for him.

In the admissions building, Molly sits in a wooden chair facing her interviewer, Miss Plum. Miss Plum teaches composition and cross-country skiing.

"You asked if I believe in *aluminum?*" Molly asks.

"Yes, dear. Uh-huh, I did," Miss Plum says.

"Well, I suppose I'd have to *believe* in it," Molly says.

❧

Annie has a large cardboard file that holds compartmentalized information on the schools they're visiting. The rules and regulations for one school are put together in what is meant to look like an American passport. In the car's backseat, Molly flips through the book annoyed.

"You can't do anything in this place!" she says. "The things on your walls have to be framed and you can only cover sixty percent of the wall space. You can't wear jeans." Molly gasps. "And you have to eat breakfast!" Molly tosses the small book onto the floor, on top of the ice scraper. She gazes glumly out the window at an orchard. She is sick of the cold. She is sick of discussing her "interests." White fields curve by. Her life is out there somewhere, fleeing from her while she is in the backseat of this stupid car. Her life is never going to be hers. She thinks of it raining, back home in the canyon, the rain falling upon the rain. Her legs itch and her scalp itches. She has never been so bored. She thinks that the worst thing she has done so far in her life was to lie in a hot bath one night, smoking a cigarette and saying *I hate God.* That was the very worst thing. It's pathetic. She bangs her knees irritably against the front seat.

"You want to send me far enough away," she says to her parents. "I mean, it's the other side of the dumb continent. Maybe I don't even want to do this," she says.

She looks at the thick sky holding back snow. She doesn't
hate God anymore. She doesn't even think about God. Anybody who would let a kid choke on a piece of bread . . .

❦

The next school has chapel four times a week and an
indoor hockey rink. In the chapel, two fir trees are held in
wooden boxes. Wires attached to the ceiling hold them upright.
It is several weeks before Christmas.

"When are you going to decorate them?" Molly asks Shirley, her guide. Shirley is handsome and rather horrible. The
soles of her rubber boots are a bright, horrible orange. She looks
at Molly.

"We don't decorate the trees in the chapel," she says.

Molly looks at the tree stumps bolted into the wooden
boxes. Beads of sap pearl golden on the bark.

"This is a very old chapel," Shirley says. "See those pillars?
They look like marble, but they're just pine, painted to look like
marble." She isn't being friendly, she's just saying what she
knows. They walk out of the chapel, Shirley soundlessly, on her
horrible orange soles.

"Do you play hockey?" she asks.

"No," Molly says.

"Why not?"

"I like my teeth," Molly says.

"You *do*," Shirley says in mock amazement. "Just kidding,"
she says. "I'm going to show you the hockey rink anyway. It's
new. It's a big deal."

Molly sees Tom and Annie standing some distance away
beneath a large tree draped with many strings of extinguished
lights. Her mother's back is to her, but Tom sees her and waves.

41

Molly follows Shirley into the cold, odd air of the hockey rink. No one is on the ice. The air seems distant, used up. On one wall is a big painting of a boy in a hockey uniform. He is in a graceful, easy posture, skating alone on bluish ice, skating toward the viewer, smiling. He isn't wearing a helmet. He has brown hair and wide golden eyes. Molly reads the plaque beneath the painting. His name is Jimmy Watkins and he had died six years before at the age of seventeen. His parents had built the rink and dedicated it to him.

Molly takes a deep breath. "My sister, Martha, knew him," she says.

"Oh yeah?" Shirley says with interest. "Did your sister go here?"

"Yes," Molly says. She frowns a little as she lies. Martha and Jimmy Watkins of course know each other. They know everything but they have secrets too.

The air is not like real air in here. Neither does the cold seem real. She looks at Jimmy Watkins, bigger than life, skating toward them on his black skates. It is not a very good painting. Molly thinks that those who love Jimmy Watkins must be disappointed in it.

"They were very good friends," Molly says.

"How come you didn't tell me before your sister went here?"

Molly shrugs. She feels happy, happier than she has in a long time. She has brought Martha back from the dead and put her in school. She has given her a room, friends, things she must do. It can go on and on. She has given her a kind of life, a place in death. She has freed her.

"Did she date him or what?" Shirley asks.

"It wasn't like that," Molly says. "It was better than that."

42

She doesn't want to go much further, not with this girl whom she dislikes, but she goes a little further.

"Martha knew Jimmy better than anybody," Molly says.

She thinks of Martha and Jimmy Watkins being together, telling each other secrets. They will like each other. They are seventeen and fourteen, living in the single moment that they have been gone.

❦

Molly is with her parents in the car again on a winding road, going through the mountains. Tonight they will stay in an inn that Annie has read about and tomorrow they will visit the last school. Several large rocks, crusted with dirty ice, have slid upon the road. They are ringed with red cones and traffic moves slowly around them. The late low sun hotly strikes the windshield.

"Bear could handle those rocks," Molly says. "Bear would go right over them."

"Oh, that truck," Annie says.

"That truck is an ecological criminal," Tom says.

"Big Bad Bear," Molly says.

Annie shakes her head and sighs. Bear is innocent. Bear is only a machine, gleaming in a dark garage.

Molly can't see her parents' faces. She can't remember the way they looked when she was little. She can't remember what she and Martha last argued about. She wants to ask them about Martha. She wants to ask them if they are sending her so far away so that they can imagine Martha is just far away too. But she knows she will never ask such questions. There are secrets now. The dead have their secrets and the living have their secrets with the dead. This is the way it must be.

❧

Molly has her things. And she sets them up each night in the room she's in. She lays a little scarf upon the bureau first, and then her things upon it. Painted combs for her hair, a little dish for her rings. They are the only guests at the inn. It is an old rambling structure on a lake. In a few days, the owner will be closing it down for the winter. It's too cold for such an old place in the winter, the owner says. He had planned to keep it open for skating on the lake when he first bought it and had even remodeled part of the cellar as a skate room. There is a bar down there, a wooden floor, and shelves of old skates in all sizes. Window glass runs the length of one wall just above ground level and there are spotlights that illuminate a portion of the lake. But winter isn't the season here. The pipes are too old and there are not enough guests.

"Is this the deepest lake in the state?" Annie asks. "I read that somewhere, didn't I?" She has her guidebooks, which she examines each night. Everywhere she goes, she buys books.

"No," the inn's owner says. "It's not the deepest, but it's deep. You should take a look at that ice. It's beautiful ice."

He is a young man, balding, hopelessly proud of his ice. He lingers with them, having given them thick towels and new bars of soap. He offers them venison for supper, fresh bread and pie. He offers them his smooth, frozen lake.

"Do you want to skate?" Tom asks his wife and daughter. Molly shakes her head.

"No," Annie says. She takes a bottle of Scotch from her suitcase. "Are there any glasses?" she asks the man.

"I'm sorry," the man says, startled. He seems to blush. "They're all down in the skate room, on the bar." He gives a slight nod and walks away.

Tom goes down into the cellar for the glasses. The skates, their runners bright, are jumbled upon the shelves. The frozen lake glitters in the window. He pushes open the door and there it is, the ice. He steps out onto it. Annie, in their room, waits without taking off her coat, without looking at the bottle. Tom takes a few quick steps and then slides. He is wearing a suit and tie, his good shoes. It is a windy night and the trees clatter with the wind and the old inn's sign creaks on its chains. Tom slides across the ice, his hands pushed out, then he holds his hands behind his back, going back and forth in the space where the light is cast. There is no skill without the skates, he knows, and probably no grace without them either, but it is enough to be here under the black sky, cold and light and moving. He wants to be out here. He wants to be out here with Annie.

From a window, Molly sees her father on the ice. After a moment, she sees her mother moving toward him, not skating, but slipping forward, making her way. She sees their heavy awkward shapes embrace.

Molly sees them, already remembering it.

LU-LU

❦

HEATHER WAS SITTING WITH THE DUNES, DON AND
Debbie, beside their swimming pool. The Dunes were old.
Heather, who lived next door to the Dunes in a little rented
house, was young and desperate. They were all suntanned and
drinking gin and grapefruit juice, trying to do their best by the
prolifically fruiting tree in the Dunes's back yard. The grapefruits were organic, and pink inside. They shone prettily by the
hundreds between leaves curled and bumpy and spotted from
spider mite and aphid infestation.

Before Heather and the Dunes on a glass-topped table was
the bottle of gin, two thirds gone, three grapefruits, and a hand
juicer. The bottle had a picture of a little old lady on the label
who gazed out at them sternly. Beneath the table, their knees
were visible, Heather's young dimpled ones and the Dunes's
knobby ones. The knees looked troubled, even baffled, beneath
the glass.

"We could take her to Mexico," Don said. "Lu-Lu would love Mexico, I bet." He was wearing a dirty blue billed cap with a fish leaping on it.

"Not Baja, though," Debbie said. Her left arm was bandaged from where she'd burnt it on the stove. "Too many RVs there. All those old geezers with nothing better to do in their twilight years than to drive up and down Baja. They'd flatten Lu-Lu in a minute."

"I've heard that those volcanic islands off Bahia Los Angeles are full of snakes," Heather said.

The Dunes looked at her, shocked.

After a moment, Debbie said, "Lu-Lu wouldn't like that at all."

"She don't know any other snakes," Don added.

He poured more gin in all the glasses.

"Do you remember tequila, my dear?" he said to Debbie. He turned his old wrinkled face towards her.

"The beverage of Mexico," Debbie said solemnly.

"On the back of each label is a big black crow," Don said. "You can see it real good when the liquor's gone."

"The Mexicans are a morbid people," Debbie said.

"What I like best about snakes," Heather said, "is the way they move without seeming to. They *move*, but they seem to be moving *in place*. Then suddenly, they're *gone*." She snapped her fingers wetly.

"That's the thing you like best about 'em?" Don said morosely. "Better things than that to like."

Heather looked at her fingers. How did they get so damp, she wondered.

"We got inquiries as far away as San Diego, did we tell you?" Don said. "San Diego wants her real bad."

Debbie raised her chin high and shook her head back and

forth. The stringy tendons in her neck trembled. "Never!" she said. "People would stare and make comments." She shuddered. "I can hear them!"

"She's got second sight, Debbie has," Don confided to Heather. "It don't use her as a vehicle much though."

Debbie had shut her eyes and was wobbling back and forth in her chair. "San Diego!" She groaned. "A cement floor. A room with nothing in it but Lu-Lu. Nothing! No pictures, no plants . . . and people staring at her through the glass. There's a little sign telling about her happy life here in Tampa and a little about her personality, but not much, and her dimensions and all . . . And I can see one big fat guy holding an ice-cream sandwich in one hand and a little girl by the other and he's saying, "Why that thing weighs fifteen pounds more than Daddy!" Debbie gave a little yelp and dug in her ears with her fingers.

"Second sight's no gift," Don said.

"We're so old," Debbie wailed.

Don tapped the elbow of her good arm solicitously and nodded at her drink.

"We're so old," Debbie said, taking a sip. "Can't take care of ourselves nor the ones we love."

"And Heather here is young," Don said. "Don't make no difference."

"We live in the wrong time, just like Lu-Lu," Debbie said.

"Lu-Lu should have lived in the Age of Reptiles," Heather said slowly. Speaking seemed to present certain problems. She looked at the stern old lady on the gin bottle.

"She would have loved it," Don said.

"Those were the days," Debbie said. "Days of doomed grandeur."

"You know what I was reading about the other day," Don said. "I was reading about the Neanderthals."

49

Debbie looked at Don proudly. Heather scratched her tanned shoulder. The sun beat down on the crooked part in her hair. Why has love eluded me, she wondered.

"They weren't us, I read. They were a whole different species. But we're the only species that are supposed to have souls, am I right? But the Neanderthals, it turned out, buried their dead Neanderthals with bits of food and flint chips and such, and even flowers. They found the graves."

"Now how could they know there were flowers?" Debbie said.

"I forget," Don said impatiently. "I'm seventy-six, I can't remember everything." He thought for a moment. "They got ways," he said.

Debbie Dune was silent. She smoothed the little skirt of her bathing suit.

"My point is that those things might not have had souls but they *thought* they had souls."

"That's a very pretty story," Heather said slowly.

The Dunes looked at her.

"The flowers and all," Heather said.

"I don't know what you're saying, Don," Debbie said politely.

"What I'm saying," Don said, "is who's to say what's got a soul and what hasn't."

"Another thing I like about snakes," Heather said, "is the way they can occupy themselves for long stretches of time doing nothing."

"I think," Debbie said, "that what it boils down to soul-wise is simple. If things cry, they got souls. If they don't, they don't."

"Lu-Lu don't cry," Don said.

"That's right," Debbie said pluckily.

"May I get some more ice?" Heather asked.

"Oh, that's a good idea, honey. Do get some more ice," Debbie said.

Heather stood up and carefully skirting the swimming pool, made her way into the kitchen. Lu-Lu was there, drinking from a pan of milk.

"Hello, Lu-Lu," Heather said. Deaf as a post, she thought.

She opened the freezer and took out a tray of ice. She looked inside the refrigerator. There was a dozen eggs and a box of shredded wheat. I should do something for these poor old people, Heather thought. Make them a quiche or something. She nibbled on a biscuit of shredded wheat and watched Lu-Lu drink her milk. Lu-Lu stared at her as she watched.

Heather walked outside. It was hot. The geraniums growing from Crisco cans looked peaked.

"Whoops," Debbie said. "I guess we need more gin now with all this ice."

"This is a difficult day for us," Don said. "It is a day of decision."

"The gin's right on the counter there beneath the emergency phone numbers," Debbie said.

Heather went back into the kitchen. Lu-Lu was still working away at shoveling the milk in.

"Lu-Lu's eating," Heather said, outside again.

"She don't eat much," Don said.

"No, she don't," Debbie said. "But she does like her rats. You know when she swallows a rat, she keeps it in her gullet for a while and that rat is fine. That rat's snug as if it were in its own little hole."

"That rat's oblivious," Don said. "That rat thinks it might even have escaped."

"Her gullet's like a comfy little waiting room to the chamber of horrors beyond it," Debbie said.

"You know in Mexico, in that big zoo in Mexico City, once

a month they feed the boas and everybody turns out to watch. They feed 'em live chickens."

"*Such* a morbid people," Debbie said.

Heather looked across the Dunes's yard into the yard of her little rented house. Her diaphanous nightie hung on the clothesline, barely moving. Time to go, Heather thought. She sat in her chair, chewing on her sun-blistered lip.

Lu-Lu slithered toward them. She placed her spadelike head on Debbie's knee.

"Poor dear doesn't know what's going to happen next," Debbie said.

"We know neither the time nor the hour," Don said. "None of us." He peered through the glass-topped table at Lu-Lu. "Is she clouding up again?"

"She molted less than four months ago," Debbie said. "It's your eyes that are clouding up."

"She looks kind of milky to me," Don said.

"Don't you wish!" exclaimed Debbie. She winked at Heather. "Don gets the biggest kick out of Lu-Lu shedding her skin."

Don grinned shyly. He took off his billed cap and put it back on again.

"We got her skins hanging up in the lanai," Debbie said to Heather. "Have you seen them?"

Heather shook her head. They all three got up and lurched toward the lanai, a small screened room looking out over where they had been. Lu-Lu followed behind. There, thumb-tacked double-up to the mildewed ceiling were half a dozen chevron-patterned gray and papery skins rustling and clicking in the hot breeze.

"In order to do this really right, you'd need a taller room," Debbie said. "I've always wanted a nice tall room and I've never gotten one. With a nice tall room they could hang in all their glory."

"There's nothing prettier than Lu-Lu right after she molts," Don said. "She's so shiny and new!"

Heather went over to Lu-Lu's old skins. There were Lu-Lu's big empty mouth and eyes. Heather pushed her face closer and sniffed. The skins smelled salty, she thought. Then she thought that they couldn't possibly smell like anything that she could remember.

"They got a prettier sound than those tinny wind chimes," Don said. "Anybody can buy themselves one of those. What's the sense of it?"

"I almost called Lu-Lu Draco, but I'm glad I didn't," Debbie said.

"Draco would have been a big mistake all right," Don agreed.

"You'll never guess what Don used to be," Debbie said.

Heather felt sleepy and anxious at the same time. She took several tiny, restless steps.

"He was a pastry chef," Debbie said.

Heather looked at the Dunes. Never would she have imagined Don Dune to be a pastry chef.

The disclosure seemed to exhaust Debbie. Her good arm paddled through the air toward Don. "I have to go to bed now," she said.

"My dear," Don said, crooking his elbow gallantly in her direction.

Heather followed them into their small, brown bedroom. Everything was brown. It seemed cool and peaceful. Lu-Lu remained on the lanai, wrapped around a hassock.

Heather turned back the sheets and the Dunes crawled in, wearing their bathing suits.

"When I was a little girl," Debbie said, "nothing was more horrible to me than having to go to bed while it was still light."

Don took off his cap and patted his head. "Even my hair feels drunk," he said.

"I would like to take Lu-Lu and make a new life for myself," Heather announced. "I can't wait any longer."

"It's not good to wait too much," Don said.

The Dunes lay in bed, the dark sheets pulled up to their chins.

"If you go off with Lu-Lu, you've got to love her good, because Lu-Lu's got no way of showing she loves you back," Debbie said.

"Snakes ain't demonstrative as a rule," Don added. "They've got no obvious way of showing attachment."

"She'll be able to recognize your footsteps after awhile," Debbie said.

Heather was delighted.

"Will she get into my car, do you think?" Heather asked.

"Lu-Lu's a good rider," Debbie said. "A real good rider. I always wanted to drive her into a nice big desert, but I never did."

"We'll find a desert," Heather said with enthusiasm. She wouldn't wait a moment longer.

"Debbie don't think she's ever wanted much, but she has," Don said. He sighed.

"We'd better get started," Heather said. She smoothed the sheet and tucked it in under the mattress.

"Bless you, honey," Debbie said drowsily.

"Spoon a little jelly in Lu-Lu's milk sometimes," Don said. "She enjoys that."

Heather left the bedroom and hurried across the yard to her driveway. Her car stalled several times as she coaxed it across the two lawns toward the Dunes's swimming pool. She opened all the doors to the car, and then the doors to the Dunes's house. She was rushing all around inside herself. Lu-Lu stared fixedly at her from the lanai.

"Come, Lu-Lu!" Heather cried.

Already her own house looked as if it had been left for good. The nightie dangled on the clothesline. Leave it there, she thought. Ugly nightie with its yearnings. She wondered if Lu-Lu would want dirt for their trip. She found Don Dune's shovel and threw some earth into the back seat of the car. She didn't know how she was going to get Lu-Lu in. She sat on the hood of the car and stared at Lu-Lu. Dusk was growing into dark. How do you beckon to something like this, she wondered; something that can change everything, your life.

GURDJIEFF IN THE SUNSHINE STATE

THIS IS ENDLESS, G. THINKS. HE IS SITTING AT A table in the lounge area of a roller-skating rink in Florida, watching the children skate. On the table are french fries, cheese-filled pretzel logs, two chicken enchiladas and a glass of water with no ice. *How strange that I am in this place,* G. thinks. He wishes, in a way, that he were back in Atlantis, but there are so many Germans there! With those panting, slobbering dogs all trained to sniff out pharmaceuticals! *Try to enjoy Florida,* he commands himself. Outside there are oranges and pelicans and snake farms. And sharks' teeth! Impossible to walk along the beaches of Florida without picking up sharks' teeth between one's toes. Inside, he is very comfortable in the air conditioning. He wears a heavy overcoat with a tightly curled lamb's-wool collar and a Cossack cap. In his pocket are forty-seven rolls of film. *I've got to get these things developed,* G. thinks. There comes a point . . .

❦

There are a hundred preadolescents with clear blue eyes and cute knees tearing around the rink at great speed. The preadolescents make G. feel tired. *Questions, questions, questions,* G. thinks. It's a blessing answers are not required. G. strokes his large mustache. *A baked potato is more intelligent than a raw potato,* he muses. *I think.*

❦

G. feels a little vague. He's been thinking about the Hindus too much. He would like to go to India again but believing in the Eternal Now as he must, he's afraid of the Thugs. The British stamped out Thuggee in 1840 but that doesn't help G. The Thugs strangled travelers with scarves and threw them down wells. They did not kill everybody. There were certain restrictions. They did not strangle women or lepers or the blind or the mutilated or anyone driving a cow or stonecutters or shoemakers. G. counts these types on his fingers. He is none of these people. He shudders. *Better stay away from India,* he thinks. G. is afraid of Thugs. He also fears mud. The dreams he has about mud he wouldn't tell a living soul. *Better squash this kind of thinking,* G. decides.

❦

G. was used to having dead people around him. He was used to admirers saying, "All the people around you seem dead." He got used to that kind of praise. No one says anything like that to him here. No one seems to notice him.

The music is deafening. Sometimes a song is played that is a little slower but no less loud than the others and the preadolescents dance to it on their roller skates. G. loves dancing. He taps his foot and strokes his mustache. The dark waters of the Tab imprisoned in the paper cup jiggle on the tabletop. *I'm in Florida!* he thinks. He loves Florida, the cold center of it. *Dance the orange,* he says enthusiastically. *Uh-oh,* he thinks. *That belongs to someone else. That German poet. Those Germans are everywhere,* he thinks with irritation. In Mexico, they were in the pyramids, in the swimming pools, in the markets buying tin lamps. In Paris, they were in the Louvre, applying Freudian theory to da Vinci, standing in front of "The Holy Family," yelling, "I see the vulture, do you see the vulture!" They were even on the Riviera, eating trout. G. has to admit, however, that they make wonderful cars. *Those BMWs,* he thinks, with a thrill of pleasure. He wishes he could dump his stupid car somewhere and get a Jaguar. *Dance the orange,* he recalls with embarrassment. He blushes but no one can tell.

Katherine Mansfield comes up to the table and sits down, gloomy as ever. He does not offer her a cigarette. She may be asleep but one never knows. No need to insult her. He smiles. *Isn't it great to be young,* he says, indicating the skaters, just making chitchat. Katherine Mansfield looks at him with consternation. *When will she cheer up!* G. sighs. He bends forward. *Impossibility is sign of truth,* he hisses. *That which can be expressed cannot be true. How many times I have to tell you that!* "I was a writer," Katherine Mansfield says with dignity. She goes away.

❧

G. longs for a glass of Calvados from one of those twenty-seven bottles he found covered over with a mixture of lime, sand and finely chopped straw when he was digging a pit in his cellar to preserve carrots. Gee, that would taste good. This Tab doesn't taste real. He would like a glass of Calvados and he would like one of those big rugs the Thugs made after their rehabilitation. Those men changed their lives. From stranglers, they became weavers. Oh, G. has always wanted one of those rugs! What a conversation piece!

❧

The children are flying around like dervishes. Crazy kids. G. stares at them, absorbed, intent. His jaw begins to ache. He lights a cigarette, smokes, coughs, yawns, laughs. Jesus never laughed. *Poor guy,* G. thinks. A small boy in silk shorts, a shirt covered with arcane lettering and black roller skates with huge green wheels floats up to the wall and crashes into it. G. laughs. *I know what that feels like,* he thinks. *That tree outside Fontaine-bleau did not move one inch. Be careful,* he shouts to the small boy, laughing. *Or you'll be like me, a bit of live meat in a clean bed.* He is asked to leave.

❧

G. walks along the beach. *What I need is to get into the ocean,* he thinks. But there is only the Gulf. He's taking it all in. *I'm in Florida!* he thinks. His great shaven dome gleams in the sun. He approaches the water, swishes his right foot in it. It's tepid, the water. *I'm not being spontaneous enough,* G. worries. *I should just run right in, catch a wave, bodysurf back out. Or maybe I should just do a little skim-boarding in the shallows.* Under his overcoat he wears a pair of red shorts, not Nantucket reds but close to the color of Nantucket reds. When G.'s granny was dying, she said to G.: *In Life Never Do As Others Do.* On her deathbed, her last words, imagine! Saying that to a little kid.

❧

G. sits on the shore. It is January, G. was born in January. It's getting dark. *Uh-oh,* G. thinks. Down the beach comes a black carriage drawn by an old horse guided by a drunken coachman. *This is very familiar,* G. thinks. His dark eyes glitter as he regards the spectacle. Everything is exactly right. The coachman is ignorant and disheveled, the horse is mistreated and spiritless, the carriage is in need of repair. *An exact cosmic actualization of my most favorite metaphor,* G. exclaims with delight. *Here!* The carriage stops in front of G. There is *no way* G. is going to get into that carriage. Nonchalantly, he bends down and picks up a little piece of coral and sails it out over the water. Plip Plip Plip Plip PlipPlipPlip it goes. Cursing, the coachman urges his horse onward. The horse doesn't move. The coachman climbs down from the carriage and starts beating the horse, punching him in the neck, kicking him in the ribs. Suddenly a German rushes out from behind a clump of sea oats and stays the violent coachman's hand. It is Nietzsche, Friedrich Nietzsche! He throws his arms around the horse's head and goes insane on the spot. No question about it, completely insane. He is taken off, babbling, in the broken-down carriage. G. looks after them, startled, but then remembers that it *is* January. *Nice forehead,* he has to admit. G. is alone once more on the darkening shore. Completely alone. But nothing has been lost. Nothing.

BROMELIADS

JONES'S GRANDCHILD IS EIGHT DAYS OLD. HE AND his wife have not been sent a picture of the baby and although they have spoken with their daughter several times on the telephone they do not have a very good idea of what the child looks like. It seems very difficult to describe a new baby. Jones has seen quite a few new babies in his years of serving a congregation and he has held them and gazed into their large sweet eyes. These experiences, however, cannot help him picture *this* child, his only grandchild, this harmonious and sweet thought that he carries in his mind, green and graceful as a fern.

Jones and his wife had no idea that their daughter was going to have a baby. They had seen her six months ago and she had mentioned nothing about a baby. Several days after the birth, her husband had called them with the news.

Jones lies awake in the night, troubled by this. His wife

twists restlessly beside him. She has been having great difficulty sleeping lately. Sleep is full of impossible chores, unending labors. She is so tired but her body cannot find any rest. She feels cold. She gets up and goes into the bathroom and runs hot water over her hands. She pats her cheeks with the hot water. While she is in the bathroom, Jones goes down to the kitchen and boils water for two cups of tea. He makes up a tray of tea and lemon peel and peanut butter cookies. He and his wife sit in bed and sip the tea. She does not feel so cold now. She feels better. They talk about the little baby. Their daughter has told them that the baby has a nice mouth and pale brown hair.

"Pale brown," Jones says enthusiastically.

His wife wants very much to travel down and see the baby even though the trip is over a thousand miles. She wants to leave as soon as possible, the next day. She is very insistent about this.

Jones walks with his daughter in the woods behind her small house. She is pointing out the various species of bromeliads that flourish there. The study of bromeliads is his daughter's most recent enthusiasm. She is a thin, hasty, troubling girl with exact and joyless passions. She lopes silently ahead of Jones through the dappled lemon-smelling woods. The trees twist upwards. Only the tops of them are green. She is wearing a faded brief bikini, and there are bruises on her legs and splashes of paint on the bikini. There is a cast to the flesh, a slender delicate mossy line on her flat stomach, extending down from the navel. It is a wistful, insubstantial line.

The baby is napping back in the little cypress cottage that Jones's daughter and her husband are renting. Jones's wife is napping too. Earlier that morning Jones had gone to the super-

market and bought food for his wife that was rich in iron.
Perhaps she is tired because of an iron deficiency. Jones had
gone through the aisles, pushing a cart. There was an arrange-
ment in the front of the cart which could be pushed back into
a seat, two spaces through which a child could put his legs. Many
children were in the store, transported in these carts. Some of
them smiled at Jones with their small prim teeth. Jones had
bought eggs, green vegetables, liver, molasses and nuts. When
he returned, his wife had wanted nothing. She sat in her slip,
on a cot in the baby's room.

Jones fanned his face with a roadmap. "I'd like to treat us
all to a strawberry soda later," he said.

"Oh that would be very refreshing," his wife replied. "That
would be very nice, but right now, I think I'd just like to watch
the baby while she sleeps." She had moved her lips in a gesture
for Jones.

Jones had kissed her forehead. He had gone outside. His
daughter is walking there, padding through the rich mulch of
oak leaves with her bare feet.

"*Neoregelia spectabilis,*" his daughter says. "*Aechmea ful-
gens.*" There are hundreds of bromeliads, some growing in the
crotches of trees, others clinging epiphytically to each other,
massed across the ground. His daughter identifies them all.
"*Hohenbergia stellata,*" she says. They are thick glossy plants with
extraordinary flowers. Their rosettes of leaves are filled with
water.

"Perhaps mother should drink some of this," she says,
waggling her finger in the cups of a heavily clustered bromeliad.
The water is brown and acrid. Jones stares at his daughter. She
shrugs. "They call it 'tea,' " she says. Her face is remote and
bony. "I don't know," she says, and begins gnawing on her nails.

The sunlight falls down through the branches of the cedars

and the live oaks as though through measured slats in a greenhouse.

"Bromeliads are fascinating," she says abruptly. "They live on nothing. Just the air and the wind. The rain brings dust and bird excrement to feed them. Leaves from trees fall into their cups and break down into nutrients. They must be one of God's favorites. One doesn't have to do anything for them. They take no care whatsoever."

Jones was saddened by her words.

Jones's daughter is preparing dinner. She darts from kitchen to porch, nursing the baby as she lays out the silverware. The cottage is dark and hot. Everyone is very hot. The dog drinks continually from a large bowl set on the floor. Jones fills it when it is empty and the dog continues to drink. The dog's tongue seems impossibly long and unwieldy. Jones stands in the kitchen, by the refrigerator, filling a glass with ice cubes. His daughter is at the stove, stirring the white sauce with a whisk. The baby has fallen asleep, her cheek riding on her mother's tanned breast, her mouth a lacy bubble of milk. Jones would like to hug them both, his daughter and her child. He does. The baby wakens with a squeak.

"Daddy," Jones's daughter says. She hunches her shoulders.

"What are you thinking about, love?" Jones asks.

"The white sauce," she says. She holds the back of the spoon to her lips. Her lower lip is split and burnt by the sun. She has brushed her brown hair straight back from her forehead and a rim of skin just below the hairline is burnt raw too. Jones stands beside her.

"It's too hot in the kitchen, Daddy, please," she says.

Jones walks to the porch with the glass of ice and gives it

to his wife. She has a craving for ice. She chews it most of the day. "What is it that my body wants?" she asks, her teeth grinding the ice.

Jones's son-in-law arrives with a bottle of gin and makes everyone a gimlet with fresh limes from a tree which is visible from the house. The tree is in fruit and blossom at the same time.

"Isn't that peculiar?" Jones remarks.

"It's wonderful!" his wife says. "I understand that. It's beautiful!"

For a moment, Jones fears that she will cry.

Jones's daughter has prepared a very nice meal. The sun has vanished, leaving the sky cerise. The color pouring through the porch, however, is yellow. Jones's wife wears a gay yellow silk blouse. It is the shade of the tropical south, of the summer sundown, a color that brings no light. They all prepare to sit down. Jones's son-in-law looks concernedly at his hands.

"Excuse me," he says, "I must wash my hands." He is a blond, affable young man, very composed. He recognizes everyone in some way. There is in him a polite and not too inaccurate recognition of everything. He is a somnolent, affectionate young man.

Jones and his wife and daughter sit down at the table.

"Every time he has to take a leak, he gives me that crap about his hands," Jones's daughter says.

Jones is uncorking the wine. He coughs.

"Every time," his daughter says. "It drives me crazy."

Her hands knock angrily against the plates. Her husband

returns. She won't look at his face. Her eyes are fixed somewhere on his chest. She thrusts her face forward as though she is going to fall against his chest.

Jones's wife says, "I hope you take photographs of the baby. There can never be enough pictures. When one looks back, there are hardly any pictures at all."

❦

The night before Jones and his wife are to return home, Jones wakes abruptly from a sound sleep. He hastily puts on his bathrobe and moves through the strange room. He senses that he has fallen, into this room, into, even, his life. He feels very much the weight of this moment which seems without resolution. He is in the present, perfectly reconciled to the future but cut off from the past. It is the present that Jones has fallen into.

He walks to the baby's crib and she is fine, she is there, sleeping. Jones moves a chair up beside the crib. The baby wakes when the morning comes. She begins to cry. Jones's daughter does not come into the room. She has been gone from them now for hours.

Jones can no longer think about his daughter with any confidence. His head sweats. The sweat runs down his cheeks. *That things so extreme and scattering bright . . .* a line from Donne, those are the words which murmur in his mind. There are no other words in his mind.

❦

A letter from Jones's daughter arrives several days later. It is mailed from a little town in the west and the postmark is so large that it has almost obliterated the address. His daughter writes, "I am not well but I will get better if I can only have some time." She does not mention the baby.

Everyone agrees that Jones and his wife should care for the baby. She is weaned easily. She is a healthy, good baby.

Jones's son-in-law is very apologetic. He folds his hands behind his back and bends slightly when he looks at the baby. He hums softly, abstractly, a visiting relative.

❦

Months pass. The baby is five months old now. She is wearing bright blue overalls and a red turtleneck shirt. She is sitting on the floor and wants to take off one of her shoes. She struggles with the shoe. She cannot think of requesting or demanding assistance in this. She tugs and tugs.

Jones and the baby sit with Jones's wife in the hospital where she has been recently committed for tests. There is something wrong with her blood, it seems. She is not in a ward. She is just here for tests and she is in a stylish wing where she is allowed to wear her own clothes and even make a cup of tea on the hotplate. She bends now and unties the baby's shoe and holds it in her hand. The baby isn't wearing socks. Jones had just done a washing and none of the socks was dry. His wife feels the baby's toes to find out if they are warm. They seem warm.

Jones wiggles the baby's largest toe. "That's Crandlehurst," he says. He invents silly names for the baby's toes.

The baby looks severely at the toe and then stops looking at it without moving her eyes. Jones cannot think of names for all the baby's toes. No fond and foolish names flower in his brain. No room! His brain, instead, hums hotly with weeds, the weedy metaphors of doctors. *The white cells may be compared to the defending foot soldiers who engage the attacking enemy in mortal hand-to-hand combat and either destroy them or are themselves destroyed.*

Jones presses his finger as unobtrusively as possible against his temples. He looks at the carpeting. It is red as a valentine, redder than the baby's jersey, certainly more red than his wife's blood.

❀

Jones tells his wife how nice she looks. She is wearing a dress that he likes, one about which he has happy memories. It is very warm in the hospital. She has entered this hospital and is in another season. Outside it is winter. But the memory is one of summer, his wife in this dress with tanned pretty arms. Jones can share this with her. He shares his heart with her, all that there is. As Rilke said . . . where was it where Rilke said? *Like a piece of bread that has to suffice for two.* His heart, Jones's love. He looks at the dress. It is a trim blue and white check, slightly faded.

It is summer. They are in a little cottage, on holiday. There is a straw rug on the floor, in a complex petal pattern through which the sand falls. When the rug is lifted, the design remains, perfectly in the sand. There is a marsh. There is a row of raisins on the porch sill for the catbirds.

Jones remembers. In the mornings, the grass seemed polished with a jeweler's cloth. And Jones's wife is in this dress, rubbing the face of their daughter with the hem of this dress. Yet it cannot be this dress, surely, everything was too long ago . . .

But now the visiting hours are over. A buzzer goes off in each of the rooms. Jones and the baby return home. Jones undresses her and then dresses her again for bed. He stays in her

70

room long after she has fallen asleep. Then he goes downstairs and builds a fire in the fireplace and searches through the bookshelves for his collection of Rilke's work. The poems have been translated but the essays have not. He takes out his German grammar and begins to search for the phrase that came to him so magically earlier in the evening. Jones enjoys the feel of the grammar. He enjoys the words of another language. He needs another language, other words. He is so weary of the words he has. He enjoys the search. Is not everything the search? An hour later he comes across the passage. It is not as Jones had thought, not as he expected. Rilke is speaking not of women but of *Dinge*. He is speaking not of lovers and life, but of dolls and death. Each word rises to Jones's lips. *Was it not with a thing that you first shared your little heart, like a piece of bread that had to suffice for two? Was it not with a thing that you experienced, through it, through its existence, through its anyhow appearance, through its final smashing or enigmatic departure, all that is human, right into the depths of death?*

Jones's wife had brought the baby a toy from the hospital gift shop. It is a soft, stuffed blue elephant, eight inches high. Inside it is a music box which plays the Carousel Waltz. While the waltz plays, the elephant's trunk rotates slowly. It is a pretty toy. Jones's wife is happy that she has at last found something here that she can give the baby. For the last several days she has walked down the corridor to the gift shop. Every day, like a bird, in the warmest, strongest hour of the day, she has ventured out. When at last she saw something she wanted to buy, she felt relieved, unambiguous. She is in control, a woman buying a toy for her grandchild. There have been so many tests. She has been here for days; they will not release her. They do not know what is wrong, but it is not the worst! The first tests have been negative. It is bad but it is not the worst. What can the worst have been? She no longer needs to fear it.

She returns this day with the toy, panting a little, the veins on either side of her eyes throbbing. She sits on her bed very quietly. She can almost see the veins. Often, they seem to hover outside her head. They are out and they want to get in. They are coiled there, almost visible, knotted, stiff, a mess, tangled like a cheap garden hose. These veins, this problem, is something she could take care of, something she is certainly capable of correcting, of making tidy and functional again, if only she had the strength. She is quiet now. The noises in her face have stopped. She looks at the toy elephant. The girl who runs the gift shop has put it in a bag. A brown paper bag, crumpled as though it has been used over and over again.

Jones's wife wraps the toy in tissue paper and waits for the evening visiting hours. Jones and the baby arrive. The baby smiles at her new plaything. She is not surprised. She is too little. She raises her face to the overhead light as though it were the sun and closes her eyes.

THE LITTLE
WINTER

❦

SHE WAS IN THE AIRPORT, WAITING FOR HER FLIGHT
to be called, when a woman came to a phone near her chair. The
woman stood there, dialing, and after a while began talking in
a flat, aggrieved voice. Gloria couldn't hear everything by any
means, but she did hear her say, "If anything happens to this
plane, I hope you'll be satisfied." The woman spoke monoto-
nously and without mercy. She was tall and disheveled and
looked the very picture of someone who recently had ceased to
be cherished. Nevertheless, she was still being mollified on the
other end. Gloria heard with astounding clarity the part about
the plane being repeated several times. The woman then
slammed down the receiver and boarded Gloria's flight, flinging
herself down in a first-class seat. Gloria proceeded to the rear
and sat quietly, thinking that every person is on the brink of
eternity every moment, that the ways and means of leaving this

world are innumerable and often inconceivable. She thought in this manner for a while, then ordered a drink.

The plane pushed through the sky and the drink made her think of the way, as a child, she had enjoyed chewing on the collars of her dresses. The first drink of the day did not always bring this to mind, but frequently it did. Then she began thinking of the desert she was leaving behind and how much she liked it. Once she had liked the sea and felt she could not live without it, but now she missed it almost not at all.

The plane continued. Gloria ordered another drink, no longer resigned to believing that the woman was going to blow up the plane. Now she began thinking of her plans. She was going to visit Jean, a friend of hers, who was having a hard time—a third divorce, after all, but Jean had a lot of energy—but that was only for a day or two. Jean had a child named Gwendal. Gloria hadn't seen them for over a year, and probably wouldn't even recognize Gwendal. Then she would just keep moving around until it happened. She was thinking of buying a dog. She'd had a number of dogs but hadn't had very good luck with them. This was the thing about pets, of course, you knew that something dreadful was going to befall them, that it was not going to end well. Two of her dogs had been hit by cars, one had been epileptic and another was diagnosed early on as having hip dysplasia. She'd bought that one from the same litter Kafka's great-niece had bought hers from. Kafka's great-niece! Vets had never done very well by Gloria's dogs, much as doctors weren't doing very well by Gloria now. She thought frequently about doctors, though she wasn't going to see them anymore. Under the circumstances, she probably shouldn't acquire a dog, but she felt she wanted one. Let the dog get stuck for a change, she thought.

At the airport, Gloria rented a car. She decided to drive

until just outside Jean's town and check into a motel. Jean was a talker. A day with Jean would be enough. A day and a night would be too much. Just outside Jean's town was a monastery where the monks raised dogs. Maybe she would find her dog there tomorrow. She would go over to the monastery early in the morning and spend the rest of the day with Jean. But that was it. Other than that, there wasn't much of a plan.

The day was cloudy and there was a great deal of traffic. The land falling back from the highway was green and still. It seemed to her a slightly morbid landscape, obelisks and cemetaries, thick drooping forests, the evergreens dying from the top down. Of course there was hardly any place to live these days. A winding old road ran parallel to the highway and Gloria turned off and drove along it until she came to a group of cabins. They were white with little porches but the office was in a structure built to resemble a tepee. There was a dilapidated miniature-golf course and a wooden tower from the top of which you could see into three states. But the tower leaned and the handrail curving optimistically upward was splintered and warped, and only five steps from the ground a rusted chain prevented further ascension. Gloria liked places like this.

In the tepee, a woman in a housedress stood behind a pink formica counter. A glass hummingbird coated with greasy dust hung in one window. Gloria could smell meat loaf cooking. The woman had red cheeks and white hair, and she greeted Gloria extravagantly, but as soon as Gloria paid for her cabin the woman became morose. She gazed at Gloria glumly, as though perceiving her as one who had already walked off with the blankets, the lamp and the painting of the waterfall.

The key Gloria had been given did not work. It fit into the lock and turned, but did not do the job of opening the door. She walked back to the office and a small dog with short legs and a fluffy tail fell into step beside her. Back in the tepee, Gloria said, "I can't seem to make this key work." The smell of the meat loaf was now clangorous. The woman was old, but she came around the counter fast.

The dog was standing in the middle of the turnabout in front of the cabins.

"Is that your dog?" Gloria asked.

"I've never seen it before," the woman said. "It sure is not," she added. "Go home!" she shrieked at the dog. She turned the key in the lock of Gloria's cabin and then gave the door a sharp kick with her sneaker. The door flew open. She stomped back to the office. "Go home!" she screamed again at the dog.

Gloria made herself an iceless drink in a paper cup and called Jean.

"I can't wait to see you," Jean said. "How are you?"

"I'm all right," Gloria said.

"Tell me."

"Really," Gloria said.

"I can't wait to see you." Jean said. "I've had the most godawful time. I know it's silly."

"How is Gwendal doing?"

"She never liked Chuckie anyway. She's Luke's, you know. But she's not a bit like Luke. You know Gwendal."

Gloria barely remembered the child, who would be almost ten by now. She sipped from the paper cup and looked through the screen at the dog who was gazing over the ruined golf course to the valley beyond.

"I don't know how I manage to pick them," Jean was saying. She was talking about the last one.

"I'll be there by lunch tomorrow," Gloria said.

"Not until then! Well, we'll bring some lunch over to Bill's and eat with him. You haven't met him, have you? I want you to meet him."

Bill was Jean's first ex-husband. She had just bought a house in town where two of her old ex-husbands and her new ex-husband lived. Gloria knew she had quite a day cut out for herself tomorrow. Jean gave her directions and Gloria hung up and made herself a fresh drink in the paper cup. She stood out on the porch. Dark clouds had massed over the mountains. Traffic thundered invisibly past in the distance, beyond the trees. In the town in the valley below, there were tiny hard lights in the enlarging darkness. The light, which had changed, was disappearing, but there was still a lot of light. That's the way it was with light. If you were out in it while it was going you could still see enough for longer. When it was completely dark, Gloria said, "Well, good-night."

She woke mid-morning with a terrible headache. She was not supposed to drink but what difference did it make, really. It didn't make any difference. She took her pills. Sometimes she thought it had been useless for her to grow older. She was thirty-five. She lay in the musty cabin. Everything seemed perfectly clear. Then it seemed equivocal again. She dressed and went to the office where she paid for another night. The woman took the money and looked at Gloria worriedly as though she were already saying good-bye to the towels she had just bought, and that old willow chair with the cushion.

It began to rain. The road to the monastery was gravel and wound up the side of a mountain. There were orchards, fields of young corn . . . the rain fell upon it all in a fury. Gloria drove slowly, barely able to make out the road. She imagined it snowing out there, not rain but snow, filling everything up. She imagined thinking *it was dark now but still snowing*—a line like that, as in a story. A line like that was lovely, she thought. When she was small they had lived in a place where the little winter came first. That's what everyone called it. There was "the little winter," then there were pleasant days, sometimes weeks. Then the big winter came. She felt dreamy and cold, a little disconnected from everything. She was on the monastery's grounds now and there were wooden buildings with turreted roofs and minarets. Someone had planted birches. She parked before a sign that said *Information/Gift Shop* and dashed from the car to the door. She was laughing and shaking the water from her hair as she entered.

The situation was that there were no dogs available, or rather that the brother whose duty was the dogs, who knew about the dogs, was away and would not return until tomorrow. She could come back tomorrow. The monk who told her this had a beard and wore a soiled apron. His interest in her questions did not seem intense. He had appeared from a back room, a room that seemed part smokehouse, part kitchen. This was the monk who smoked chickens, hams and cheese. There was always cheese in this life. The monastery had a substantial mail-order business; the monks smoked things, the nuns made cheesecakes. He seemed slightly impatient with Gloria and she was aware that her questions about the dogs seemed desultory. He had given up a great deal, no doubt, in order to be here. The gift shop was crowded with half-priced icons and dog beds. In a corner there was a glass case filled with the nuns' cheesecakes. Gloria looked in there, at the stacks of white boxes.

"The Deluxe is a standard favorite," the monk said. "The Kahlua is encased in a chocolate cookie–crumb crust, the rich liquer from sunny Mexico blending naturally with the nuns' original recipe." The monk droned on as if at matins. "The Chocolate is a must for chocolate fanciers. The Chocolate Amaretto is considered by the nuns to be their pièce de résistance."

Gloria bought the Chocolate Amaretto and left. How gloomy, she thought. The experience had seemed vaguely familiar as though she had surrendered passively to it in the past. She supposed it was a belief in appearances. She put the cheesecake in the car and walked around the grounds. It was raining less heavily now, but even so her hair was plastered to her skull. She passed the chapel and then turned back and went inside. She picked up a candlestick and jammed it into her coat pocket. This place made her mad. Then she took the candlestick out and set it on the floor. Outside, she wandered around, hearing nothing but the highway, which was humming like something in her head. She finally found the kennels and opened the door and went in. This is the way she thought it would be, nothing closed to her at all. There were four dogs, all young ones, maybe three months old, German Shepherds. She watched them for a while. It would be easy to take one, she thought. She could just do it.

She drove back down the mountain into town, where she pulled into a shopping center that had a liquor store. She bought gin and some wine for Jean, then drove down to Jean's house in the valley. She felt tired. There was something pounding behind her eyes. Jean's house was a dirty peach color with a bush in front. Everything was pounding, the house, even the grass. Then the pounding stopped.

"Oh my God," Jean exclaimed. "You've brought the pièce de résistance!" Apparently everyone was familiar with the nuns' cheesecakes. Jean and Gloria hugged each other. "You look good," Jean said. "They got it all, thank God, right? The things that happen anymore . . . there aren't even names for half of what happens, I swear. You know my second husband, Andy, the one who died? He went in and he never came out again and he just submitted to it, but no one could ever figure out what *it* was. It was something complicated and obscure and the only thing they knew was that he was dying from it. It might've been some insect that bit him. But the worst thing—well, not the worst thing, but the thing I remember because it had to do with me, which is bad of me, I suppose, but that's just human nature. The worst thing was what happened just before he died. He was very fussy. Everything had to be just so."

"This is Andy," Gloria said.

"Andy," Jean agreed. "He had an excellent vocabulary and was very precise. How I got involved with him I'll never know. But he was my husband and I was devastated. I *lived* at the hospital, week after week. He liked me to read to him. I was there that afternoon and I had adjusted the shade and plumped the pillows and I was reading to him. And there he was, quietly slipping away right then, I guess, looking back on it. I was reading and I got to this part about someone being the master of a highly circumscribed universe and he opened his eyes and said, Circumscribed. What, darling? I said. And he said, Circumscribed, not circumcised . . . you said circumcised. And I said, I'm sure I didn't, darling, and he gave me this long look and then he gave a big sigh and died. Isn't that awful?"

Gloria giggled, then shook her head.

Jean's eyes darted around the room, which was in high disorder. Peeling wallpaper, cracked linoleum. Cardboard boxes everywhere. Shards of glass had been swept into one corner and a broken croquet mallet propped one window open. "So what do you think of this place?" Jean said.

"It's some place," Gloria said.

"Everyone says I shouldn't have. It needs some work, I know, but I found this wonderful man, or he found me. He came up to the door and looked at all this and I said, Can you help me? Do you do work like this? And he nodded and said, I puttah. Isn't that wonderful! I puttah . . . "

Gloria looked at the sagging floor and the windows loose in their frames. The mantel was blackened by smoke and grooved with cigarette burns. It was clear that the previous occupants had led lives of grinding boredom here and had not led them with composure. He'd better start puttahing soon, Gloria thought. "Don't marry him," she said, and laughed.

"Oh, I know you think I marry everybody," Jean said, "but I don't. There have only been four. The last one, and I mean the last, was the worst. What a rodent Chuckie was. No, he's more like a big predator, a crow or a weasel or something. Cruel, lazy, deceitful." Jean shuddered. "The best thing about him was his hair." Jean was frequently undone by hair. "He has great hair. He wears it in a sort of fifties full flat-top."

Gloria felt hollow and happy. Nothing mattered much.

"Love is a chimera," Jean said earnestly.

Gloria laughed.

"I'm pronouncing that right, aren't I?" Jean said, laughing.

"You actually bought this place?" Gloria said.

"Oh, it's crazy," Jean said, "but Gwendal and I needed a home. I've heard that *faux* is the new trend. I'm going to do it all *faux* when I get organized. Do you want to see the upstairs? Gwendal's room is upstairs. Hers is the neatest."

They went up the stairs to a room where a fat girl sat on a bed writing in a book.

"I'm doing my autobiography," Gwendal said, "but I think I'm going to change my approach." She turned to Gloria. "Would you like to be my biographer?"

Jean said, "Say hello to Gloria. You remember Gloria."

Gloria gave the girl a hug. Gwendal smelled good and had

small gray eyes. The room wasn't clean at all, but there was very little in it. Gloria supposed it was the neatest. Conversation lagged.

"Let's go out and sit on the lawn," Jean suggested.

"I don't want to," Gwendal said.

The two women went downstairs. Gloria needed to use the bathroom but Jean said she had to go outside as the plumbing wasn't all it should be at the moment. There was a steep brushy bank behind the house and Gloria crouched there. The day was clear and warm now. At the bottom of the bank, a flat stream moved laboriously around vine-covered trees. The mud glistened in the sun. Blackberries grew in the brush. This place had a lot of candor, Gloria thought.

Jean had laid a blanket on the grass and was sitting there, eating a wedge of cheesecake from a plastic plate. Gloria decided on a drink over cake.

"We'll go to Bill's house for lunch," Jean said. "Then we'll go to Fred's house for a swim." Fred was an old husband too. Gwendal's father was the only one who wasn't around. He lived in Las Vegas. Andy wasn't around either, of course.

Gwendal came out of the house into the sloppy yard. She stopped in the middle of a rhubarb patch, exclaiming silently and waving her arms.

Jean sighed. "It's hard being a single mother."

"You haven't been single for long," Gloria said.

Jean laughed loudly at this. "Poor Gwendal," she said, "I love her dearly."

"A lovely child," Gloria murmured.

"I just wish she wouldn't make up so much stuff sometimes."

"She's young," Gloria said, swallowing her drink. Really, she hardly knew what she was saying. "What *is* she doing?" she asked Jean.

Gwendal leapt quietly around in the rhubarb.

"Whatever it is, it needs to be translated," Jean said. "Gwendal needs a good translator."

"She's pretending something or other," Gloria offered, thinking she would very much like another drink.

"I'm going to put on a fresh dress for visiting Bill," Jean said. "Do you want to put on a fresh dress?"

Gloria shook her head. She was watching Gwendal. When Jean went into the house, the girl trotted over to the blanket. "Why don't you kidnap me," she said.

"Why don't you kidnap *me?*" Gloria said, laughing. What an odd kid, she thought. "I don't want to kidnap you," she said.

"I'd like to see your house," Gwendal said.

"I don't have a house. I lived in an apartment."

"Apartments aren't interesting," Gwendal said. "Dump it. We could get a van. The kind with the ladder that goes up the back. We could get a wheel cover that says *Mess with the Best, Lose like the Rest.*"

There was something truly terrifying about girls on the verge of puberty, Gloria thought. She laughed.

"You drink too much," Gwendal said. "You're always drinking something."

This hurt Gloria's feelings. "I'm dying," she said. "I have a brain tumor. I can do what I want."

"If you're dying you can do anything you want?" Gwendal said. "I didn't know that. That's a new one. So there are compensations."

Gloria couldn't believe she'd told Gwendal she was dying. "You're fat," she said glumly.

Gwendal ignored this. She wasn't all that fat. Somewhat fat, perhaps, but not grotesquely so.

"Oh, to hell with it," Gloria said. "You want me to stop drinking, I'll stop drinking."

"It doesn't matter to me," Gwendal said.

Gloria's mouth trembled. I'm drunk, she thought.

"Some simple pleasures are just a bit too simple, you know," Gwendal said.

Gloria had felt she'd been handling her upcoming death pretty well, but now she wasn't sure. In fact she felt awful. What was she doing spending what might be one of her last days sitting on a scratchy blanket in a weedy yard while a fat child insulted her? Her problem was that she had never figured out where it was exactly she wanted to go to die. Some people knew and planned accordingly. The desert, say, or Nantucket. Or a good hotel somewhere. But she hadn't figured it out. En route was the closest she'd come.

Gwendal said, "Listen, I have an idea. We could do it the other way around. Instead of you being my biographer, I'll be yours. *Gloria by Gwendal.*" She wrote it in the air with her finger. She did not have a particularly flourishing hand, Gloria noted. "Your life as told to Gwendal Crawley. I'll write it all down. At least that's something. We can always spice it up."

"I haven't had a very interesting life," Gloria said modestly. But it was true, she thought. When her parents had named her, they must have been happy. They must have thought something was going to happen now.

"I'm sure you must be having some interesting reflections, though," Gwendal said. "And if you're really dying, I bet you'll feel like doing everything once." She was wringing her hands in delight.

Jean walked toward them from the house.

"C'mon," Gwendal hissed. "Let me go with you. You didn't come all this way just to stay here, did you?"

"Gloria and I are going to visit Bill," Jean said. "Let's all go," she said to Gwendal.

"I don't want to," Gwendal said.

"If I don't see you again, good-bye," Gloria said to Gwendal.

The kid stared at her.

&

Jean was driving, turning this way and that, passing the houses of those she had once loved.

"That's Chuckie's house," Jean said. "The one with the hair." They drove slowly by, looking at Chuckie's house. "Charming on the outside but sleazy inside, just like Chuckie. He broke my heart, literally broke my heart. Well, his foot is going to slide in due time, as they say, and I want to be around for that. That's why I've decided to stay." She said a moment later, "It's not really."

They passed Fred's house. Everybody had a house.

"Fred has a pond," Jean said. "We can go for a swim there later. I always use Fred's pond. He used to own a whole quarry, can you imagine? This was before our time with him, Gwendal's and mine, but kids were always getting in there and drowning. He put up big signs and barbed wire and everything but they still got in. It got to be too much trouble, so he sold it."

"Too much trouble!" Gloria said.

Death seemed preposterous. Totally unacceptable. Those silly kids, Gloria thought. She was elated and knew that she would feel tired soon and uneasy, but maybe it wouldn't happen this time. The day was bright, clean after the rain. Leaves lay on the streets, green and fresh.

"Those were Fred's words, too much trouble. Can't I pick them? I can really pick them." Jean shook her head.

They drove to Bill's house. Next to it was a pasture with

horses in it. "Those aren't Bill's horses, but they're pretty, aren't they," Jean said. "You're going to love Bill. He's gotten a little strange but he always was a little strange. We are who we are, aren't we. He carves ducks."

Bill was obviously not expecting them. He was a big man with long hair wearing boxer shorts and smoking a cigar. He looked at Jean warily.

"This used to be the love of my life," Jean said. To Bill, she said, "This is Gloria, my dearest friend."

Gloria felt she should demur, but smiled instead. Her situation didn't make her any more honest, she had found.

"Beautiful messengers, bad news," Bill said.

"We just thought we'd stop by," Jean said.

"Let me put on my pants," he said.

The two women sat in the living room, surrounded by wooden ducks. The ducks, exquisite and oppressive, nested on every surface. Bufflehead, canvasback, scaup, blue-winged teal. Gloria picked one up. It looked heavy but was light. Shoveler, mallard, merganser. The names kept coming to her.

"I forgot the lunch so we'll just stay a minute," Jean whispered. "I was *mad* about this man. Don't you ever wonder where it all goes?"

Bill returned, wearing trousers and a checked shirt. He had put his cigar somewhere.

"I *love* these ducks," Jean said. "You're getting so good."

"You want a duck," Bill said.

"Oh yes!" Jean said.

"I wasn't offering you one. I just figured that you did." He winked at Gloria.

"Oh you," Jean said.

"Take one, take one," Bill sighed.

Jean picked up the nearest duck and put it in her lap.

"That's a harlequin," Bill said.

"It's bizarre, I love it." Jean gripped the duck tightly.

"You want a duck?" Bill said to Gloria.

"No," Gloria said.

"Oh, take one!" Jean said excitedly.

"Decoys have always been particularly abhorrent to me," Gloria said, "since they are objects designed to lure a living thing to its destruction with the false promise of safety, companionship and rest."

They both looked at her, startled.

"Oh wow, Gloria," Jean said.

"These aren't decoys," Bill said mildly. "People don't use them for decoys anymore, they use them for decoration. There are hardly anymore ducks to hunt. Ducks are on their way out. They're in a free-fall."

"Diminishing habitat," Jean said.

"There you go," Bill said.

Black duck, pintail, widgeon. The names kept moving toward Gloria, then past.

"I'm more interested in creating dramas now," Bill said. "I'm getting away from the static stuff. I want to make dramatic moments. They have to be a little less than life-sized, but otherwise it's all there . . . the whole situation." He stood up. "Just a second," he said.

Once he was out of the room, Jean turned to her. "Gloria?" she said.

Bill returned carrying a large object covered by a sheet. He set it down on the floor and took off the sheet.

"I like it so far," Jean said after a moment.

"Interpret away," Bill said.

"Well," Jean said, "I don't think you should make it too busy."

"I said interpret, not criticize," Bill said.

"I just think the temptation would be to make something like that too busy. The temptation would be to put stuff in all those little spaces."

Bill appeared unmoved by this possible judgment, but he replaced the sheet.

❀

In the car, Jean said, "Wasn't that *awful*. He should stick to ducks."

According to Bill, the situation the object represented seemed to be the acceptance of inexorable fate, this acceptance containing within it, however, a heroic gesture of defiance.

This was the situation, ideally always the situation, and it had been transformed, more or less abstractly, by Bill, into wood.

"He liked you."

"Jean, why would he like me?"

"He was flirting with you, I think. Wouldn't it be something if you two got together and we were all here in this one place?"

"Oh my *God*," Gloria said, putting her hands over her face. Jean glanced at her absent-mindedly. "I should be getting back," Gloria said. "I'm a little tired."

"But you just got here, and we have to take a swim at Fred's. The pond is wonderful, you'll love the pond. Actually, listen, do you want to go over to my parents' for lunch? Or it should be dinner, I guess. They have this big television. My mother can make us something nice for dinner."

"Your parents live around here too?" Gloria asked.

Jean looked frightened for a moment. "It's crazy, isn't it?

They're so sweet. You'd love my parents. Oh, I wish you'd talk," she exclaimed. "You're my friend. I wish you'd open up some."

They drove past Chuckie's house again. "Whose car is that now?" Jean wondered.

"I remember trying to feed my mother a spoonful of dust once," Gloria said.

"Why?" Jean said. "Tell!"

"I was little, maybe four. She told me that I had grown in her stomach because she'd eaten some dust."

"No!" Jean said. "The things they tell you when they know you don't know."

"I wanted there to be another baby, someone else, a brother or a sister. So I had my little teaspoon. Eat this, I said. It's not a bit dirty. Don't be afraid."

"How out of control!" Jean cried.

"She looked at it and said she'd been talking about a different kind of dust, the sort of dust there was on flowers."

"She was just getting in deeper and deeper, wasn't she?" Jean said. She waited for Gloria to say more but the story seemed to be over.

It was dark when she got back to the cabins. There were no lights on anywhere. She remembered being happy off and on that day, and then looking at things and finding it all unkind. It had gotten harder for her to talk, and harder to listen too, but she was alone now and she felt a little better. Still, she didn't feel right. She knew she would never be steady. It would never seem all of a piece for her. It would come and go until it stopped.

She pushed open the door and turned on the lamp beside the bed. There were three sockets in the lamp but only one bulb.

There had been more bulbs in the lamp last night. She also thought there had been more furniture in the room, another chair. Reading would have been difficult, if she had wanted to read, but she was tired of reading, tired of books. After they had told her the first time and even after they had told her the other times in different ways, she had wanted to read, she didn't want to just stand around gaping at everything, but she couldn't pick the habit up again, it wasn't the same.

The screen in the window was a mottled bluish green, a coppery, oceanic color. She thought of herself as a child with the spoonful of dust, but it was just a memory of her telling it now. She stood close to the screen, to its raw, metallic smell.

In the middle of the night she woke, soaked with sweat. Someone was just outside, she thought. Then this feeling vanished. She gathered up her things and put everything in the car. She did this all hurriedly, and then drove quickly to Jean's house. She parked out front and turned the lights off. After a few moments, Gwendal appeared. She was wearing an ugly dress and carrying a suitcase. There were creases down one side of her face as though she'd been sleeping hard before she woke. "Where to first?" Gwendal said.

What they did first was to drive to the monastery and steal a dog. Gloria suspected that fatality made her more or less invisible, and this seemed to be the case. She drove directly to the kennel, went in and walked out with a dog. She put him in the backseat and they drove off.

"We'll avoid the highway," Gloria said. "We'll stick to the back roads."

"Fine with me," Gwendal said.

Neither of them said anything for miles, then Gwendal asked, "Would you say he had drop-dead good looks?"

"He's a dog," Gloria said. Gwendal was really mixed up. She was worse than her mother, Gloria thought.

They pulled into a diner and had breakfast. Then they went to a store and bought notebooks, pencils, dog food and gin. They bought sunglasses. It was full day now. They kept driving until dusk. They were quite a distance from Jean's house. Gloria felt sorry for Jean. She liked to have everyone around her, even funny little Gwendal, and now she didn't.

Gwendal had been sleeping. Suddenly she woke up. "Do you want to hear my dream?" she asked.

"Absolutely," Gloria said.

"Someone, it wasn't you, told me not to touch this funny-looking animal, it wasn't him," Gwendal said, gesturing toward the dog. "Every time I'd pat it, it would bite off a piece of my arm or a piece of my chest. I just had to keep going 'It's cute' and keep petting it."

"Oh," Gloria said. She had no idea what to say.

"Tell me one of your dreams," Gwendal said, yawning.

"I haven't been dreaming lately," Gloria said.

"That's not good," Gwendal said. "That shows a lack of imagination. Readiness, it shows a lack of readiness maybe. Well, I can put the dreams in later. Don't worry about it." She chose a pencil and opened the notebook. "Okay," she said. "Married?"

"No."

"Any children?"

"No."

"Allergies?"

Gloria looked at her.

"Do you want to start at the beginning or do you want to work backward from the Big Surprise?" Gwendal asked.

They were on the outskirts of a town, stopped at a traffic light. Gloria looked straight ahead. Beginnings. She couldn't remember any beginnings.

"Hey," someone said. "Hey!"

She looked to her left at a dented yellow car full of young men. One of them threw a can of beer at her. It bounced off the door and they sped off, howling.

"Everyone knows if someone yells 'hey' you don't look at them," Gwendal said.

"Let's stop for the night," Gloria said.

"How are you feeling?" Gwendal asked . . . not all that solicitously, Gloria thought.

They pulled into the first motel they saw. Gloria fed the dog and had a drink while Gwendal bounced on the bed. He seemed a most equable dog. He drank from the toilet bowl and gnawed peaceably on the bed rail. Gloria and Gwendal ate pancakes in a brightly lit restaurant and strolled around a swimming pool which had a filthy rubber cover rolled across it. Back in the room, Gloria lay down on one bed while Gwendal sat on the other.

"Do you want me to paint your nails or do your hair?" Gwendal asked.

"No," Gloria said. She was recalling a bad thought she'd had once, a very bad thought. It had caused no damage, however, as far as she knew.

"I wouldn't know how to do your hair, actually," Gwendal said.

With a little training, Gloria thought, this kid could be a mortician.

That night Gloria dreamed. She dreamed she was going to the funeral of some woman who had been indifferent to her. There was no need for her to be there. She was standing with a group of people. She felt like a criminal, undetected, but she felt chosen, too, to be there when she shouldn't be. Then she was lying across the opening of a cement pipe. When she woke, she was filled with relief, knowing she would forget the dream immediately. It was morning again. Gwendal was outside by the unpleasant pool, writing in her notebook.

"*This was happiness then,*" she said, scribbling away.

"Where's the dog?" Gloria asked. "Isn't he with you?"

"I don't know," Gwendal said. "I let him out and he took off for parts unknown."

"What do you mean!" Gloria said. She ran back to the room, went to the car, ran across the cement parking lot and around the motel. Gloria didn't have any name to call the dog with. It had just disappeared without having ever been hers. She got Gwendal in the car and they drove down the roads around the motel. She squinted, frightened, at black heaps along the shoulder and in the littered grass, but it was tires, rags, tires. Cars sped by them. Along the median strip, dead trees were planted at fifty-foot intervals. The dog wasn't anywhere that she could find. Gloria glared at Gwendal.

"It was an accident," Gwendal said.

"You have your own ideas about how this should be, don't you?"

"He was kind of a distraction," Gwendal said.

Gloria's head hurt. Back in the desert, just before she had made this trip, she had had her little winter. Her heart had pounded like a fist on a door. But it was false, all false, for she had survived it.

Gwendal had the hateful notebook on her lap. It had a splatter black cover with the word *Composition* on it. "Now we can get started," she said. "Today's the day. Favorite color?" she asked. "Favorite show tune?" A childish blue barette was stuck haphazardly in her hair, exposing part of a large, pale ear.

Gloria wasn't going to talk to her.

After a while, Gwendal said, "*They were unaware that the fugitive was in their midst.*" She wrote it down. Gwendal scribbled in the book all day long and asked Gloria to buy her another one. She sometimes referred to Gloria's imminent condition as the Great Adventure.

Gloria was distracted. Hours went by and she was driving, though she could barely recall what they passed. "I'm going to pull in early tonight," she said.

The motel they stopped at late that afternoon was much like the one before. It was called the Motel Lark. Gloria lay on one bed and Gwendal sat on the other. Gloria missed having a dog. A dog wouldn't let the stranger in, she thought sentimentally. Whereas Gwendal would in a minute.

"We should be able to talk," Gwendal said.

"Why should we be able to talk?" Gloria said. "There's no reason we should be able to talk."

"You're not open is your problem. You don't want to share. It's hard to imagine what's real all by yourself, you know."

"It is not!" Gloria said hotly. They were bickering like an old married couple.

"This isn't working out," Gloria said. "This is crazy. We should call your mother."

"I'll give you a few more days, but it's true," Gwendal said. "I thought this would be a more mystical experience. I thought you'd tell me something. You don't even know about make-up. I bet you don't even know how to check the oil in that car. I've never seen you check the oil."

"I know how to check the oil," Gloria said.

"How about an electrical problem? Would you know how to fix an electrical problem?"

"No!" Gloria yelled.

Gwendal was quiet. She stared at her fat knees.

"I'm going to take a bath," Gloria said.

She went into the bathroom and shut the door. The tile

was turquoise and the stopper to the tub hung on a chain. This was the Motel Lark, she thought. She dropped the rubber stopper in the drain and ran the water. A few tiles were missing and the wall showed a gray, failed adhesive. She wanted to say something but even that wasn't it. She didn't want to say anything. She wanted to realize something she couldn't say. She heard a voice, it must have been Gwendal's, in the bedroom. Gloria lay down in the tub. The water wasn't as warm as she expected. *Your silence is no deterrent to me, Gloria,* the voice said. She reached for the hot-water faucet but it ran in cold. If she let it run, it might get warm, she thought. That's what they say. Or again, that might be it.

THE ROUTE

BALLSTON SPA, NEW YORK

We had the car so we went. We left as soon as possible for our marriage was not doing well. I am just a youngster and attractive. He is middle-aged.

I am hoping for the best from this trip. He is a chemist. We have many problems. He is working at present on a theory that shark size is dependent upon fin diameter and liver weight. Of course there are no sharks in Ballston Spa. That is one of the problems. We have never had a meeting of minds but we wed because we had good bodies.

Every day I used to wait for him to come home from the laboratory. I would make up big glasses of chocolate milk and pop-up waffles in the morning and then he would go off and I would stay in our rented bungalow by the sulphur springs and watch the old fools totter up and down the hills with their jugs and jars and paper cups. I couldn't stand to even wash my hands in that water. It turned my earrings black. But everybody was crazy about it. It made rotten coffee. The whole town smelled like a bathroom. But they were mad for it. And then at two o'clock on the dot they'd all plug in their rock tumblers and scramble my television for the rest of the afternoon.

That was the point where I would go to the Office and buy myself a bottle of Jack Daniel's giftly boxed. The liquor store was conveniently located. That was one thing about the place— nothing was anywhere if it wasn't right on top of you. I always bought my product boxed for then I could give the plastic insert of that Tennessee fellow to those various bands of children that roamed the streets of Ballston Spa. Those babies didn't have a thing, though I would bet if you went through that town today you would find them playing with those little plastic heads at least.

I would be drinking in the breakfast nook.

And just when I believed I couldn't stand it for another moment, the man who I married would rush up the walk, still in his smock, rubber-soled shoes and safety goggles and we would make frantic love.

But the zing was out of it.

Actually I didn't know him very well. He had a long dun-blond head and an absent manner.

So we were both wanting something nice to occur to us again. And Herbie at the corner Humble who's the same age as me and doesn't have a tooth in his head kindly planned the trip and made suggestions and reservations. All we had to have was the destination.

When we went we didn't leave a thing behind.

The Route

EAST WINDSOR HILL, CONNECTICUT

My first memory as a child was of a moth in my milk.

He can't recollect what his was. Nothing stands out. He had four brothers and one weird sister. Of the brood she was the only one I had the displeasure to meet, and she indirectly. We honeymooned at her cabin on Lake George. She was unmarried herself. I never even saw her photograph but I became acquainted with her washcloth full of pubic hairs—sort of hidden on a special little rod beneath the lip of the tub. Leave it to me to find it, of course. *Covered* with them as though she were going to make an afghan. Saving them like decent people would Green Stamps.

I remind him of this when I am annoyed with him. His sister. And he believes himself to be so sophisticated. What can he say? I have him there. We gobbled at each other all day. So far the trip has been dreadful. I tease his lap but he is unmoved. He dislikes attendants at toll booths. I think he would like to hurt them. He looks at them out of his heavy-lidded eyes. The attendants smile at me. Their tongues protrude a little. I am really a knockout. I could have been in films but I lack the ambition. So this first day is not a good one. We stop at a tourist home. The owner is an ancient soul. I don't know whether a little old man or a little old lady. It wore Hush Puppies and an overcoat.

Our room is warm, however, and very modern. All done in Colonial with eagles everywhere—even on the toilet tissue holder. I prepare myself and snuggle into bed, darling as a cupcake. For supper we had martinis and a soufflé but he is not happy. He sits and writes something out in a notebook. I think it is about me but when I look I realize that it concerns his goddamn sharks which he has never seen. I am an affectionate

99

person. I nibble on his back for awhile. He has never showed the slightest desire to be different. When we first met I thought he knew a lot about love but now it's clear he knows only as much as I do.

SPOTSYLVANIA, VIRGINIA

We stop for gas and the boy says, "Right over there is where Dr. Mudd was at." My husband refutes this. They glare at each other. I can't imagine what they're talking about. "He thinks we're tourists," my husband says. The boy doesn't put the gas cap back on. We remove some of our clothes because it is getting hot and we have some ice cream. The car is old and has old scratchy seats. Everywhere are trees and arsenals. He begins to talk about fishes. If I could get one starved shark, he says, just one, I could prove a lot. We are swerving along and I am having a cup of gin and tonic from our thermos. He talks and talks. I notice a clutch of freckles on his forearm that I have not seen before. They resemble a banana. A little later they bring to mind two parachutists. I am fascinated. I swear it's like going to the movies.

He is driving. This car takes a lot out of one. It is exhausting and seems to have intentions of its own. It is a Buick with big fins. I do not think about cars one way or the other but I have an opinion about this one. It has a strange odor about the right hubcap. Now I have heard that pranksters do this for a prank. They remove the hubcap and put dead fish or something awful there. Items that ladies use for their personal hygiene are popular. These same creeps will replace a perfectly good car engine with a broken-down one while you are in a restaurant or enjoying yourself somewhere. I have a suspicion that we might be victims, but I am not going to examine this further. We are traveling in a straight line but he is struggling with the wheel. His forearms bulge and sweat. He is so sorrowful. He sighs and tips the thermos to his mouth, getting the sliver of lime which is all that's left. He doesn't mind. He says chewing it keeps him awake. He is very polite and selfless. I used to be nuts for him.

That night at the La Crème de la Crème, which was clean but unexceptional, I am after him as always but he is sleeping and later when he wakes up, we take advantage of it, but he is so blue. He says, I have no dreams. I can hardly make him out in the darkness of this room but I say, Oh sweet potato, you dreamed up me. But he says Kekulé dreamt about a snake swallowing its own tail which illumined for him the structure of the benzene ring.

He talks like this. How was I to know? I was only a baby when we met. My momma was still buying my brassieres.

Otto Loewi derived his whole neurochemical concept from a dream, he says.

I am so disgusted.

ALERT, NORTH CAROLINA

This is the saddest day of my life. He was bitten by a bat. We were coming out of a restaurant after a very nice dinner and the little bugger staggered out from under a bush and fastened onto his sock. I beat it to a paste with my handbag but the act was done. I have never seen my husband under stress before. He is very calm. We went back to the motel and drank a little gin. I bought some crackers from a machine. He spoke about *N. brevirostris* and *C. milberti*, looking occasionally at his ankle where nothing could be seen. Now I am not a cerebral person if you know what I mean. I was made for better things. For example, I simply cannot be topped. Now last night I was enraged. I said to myself that never again would I have anything to do with him. We were through! And I would leave him for good in Miami. For what is in Key West? I can't imagine. Key West is merely the end of the country is all. He can go down on the sea with a fish it's all the same to me was my attitude of the night before. But life is very funny. Now he is going to die. It's very sexual. I kiss him, deeply traveling. The fillings of his teeth are like ice. There's a hint of chive and ketchup. He says, lightly, I thought, under the circumstances, I need the fluid from the brain of a suckling mouse. He knows everything and makes it all sound difficult. I am willing to go out and get it I say. He says, Or a duck embryo would do just as well. We have some more gin and he says that he's decided not to do anything about it. He goes out and around the pool of the Sun Tan Motel where we are and buys a bag of fried pork rinds from the machine. The pool has an algae problem. No one is in it. It's green as a Christmas tree. I am waiting on the bed and he comes back in all dressed up like the fellow on the Beefeater's bottle. Flowered red jerkin, hammerhead shoes and a white pointy beard. I laughed till I peed. I never knew he had this side to him.

MULLINS, SOUTH CAROLINA

This is the only Mullins I've seen though I imagine if there are others they are the same. Birds nesting in neon lettering (for birds are mean and dumb everywhere). Movie houses taken over by Chinese restaurants. Mister Softees and rags in the streets. One has to make one's own joy. To travel through America you have to be in love. I am in love again! He is twice and a half my age but sound. He has become aggressive! We've stopped for the night at one in the afternoon. He embraces my yummy legs. I hold him tight but he's a different man from yesterday. He is confident and has a feathery touch.

I become a whimpering rag.

Nonetheless, opposite the motel is an electrical supply company which we can't help but notice. He says to me, Do you recollect Gerald Gee?

Of course, I say. How could I forget. He came to our house once from the laboratory where he is supposed to be an electronics genius. He broke a dish and didn't flush the toilet.

Gerald's had his breakdown, he says. It seems he found that mathematical thinking was touching off violent erotic excitement, often culminating in orgasm.

He says he can't understand how knowing this can help him. I agree. I say it would seem to me that few are fortunate enough to get such pleasure from their work.

Dusk returns to Cash. In the windows across the street are hundreds of different lights, all lit. They've been shining all day and at night they're still on. It must cost them a fortune. And for what? What's there to use them? Who's to know?

LUGOFF, SOUTH CAROLINA

As anyone could see from any map they chose to, we have not progressed very far! Lugoff can't be more than twenty miles further.

He's torn my blouse—pushed his hand right through that chemical crap they make everything of anymore. We turned off the highway and sped down a deep black piney road. There are turkeys flying beside us. He is showing most of his mouth in a great grin. The car is rocketing away with our electricity. He stops before an abandoned house. It is really an awful place. Half built or half torn down. Ratty Johnny-Kwik erected crooked in the front yard. No door and as we run in we can see the pink Southern sky through the roof. He tells me to get on my stomach. I am so excited. The last time he suggested this, naturally I complied but then he didn't do anything. Or rather he was very quiet for awhile and then he picked up a magazine. Then he became very engrossed in that. I went out for some Campari and a green pepper sandwich. I must admit I made the acquaintance of someone there.

This time I know it will not be the same. Fate has made a shambles of us.

My eye is on the knothole.

But then we realize that we are in someone's dining room and that they are having breakfast. Their backs are to us, thank goodness. A little family eating from blue bowls. We leave immediately and no one's the wiser. The car's engine, as a matter of fact, is still running.

ATLANTA, GEORGIA

His left arm is sunburned but his face is becoming pale. Last night I felt his ribs for the first time in many months. When he spoke to me, I found that I did not know what he was saying. This is not unusual, although now we fear that what was true before has become true now because he is rabid.

When he comes around again, we discover that he is talking about sharks. I am more understanding now. I have matured a lot. He is a little boy again with the soft wet lower lip of a little boy. He wants a milkshake. We buy milkshakes and pour a pint of Scotch into them. He says that even as a little boy he wanted to invent a shark repellent.

I can see this, I say. Make a good shark repellent and the world will beat a path to your door.

His experiments have only been partially successful. The sharks keep right on eating the protected food even while they're dying. Feeder and feedee are both out of luck. Such things have to be ironed out.

Now he hasn't the time.

We kiss.

We are making it in a bank's parking lot. Santa Claus is walking back and forth. He's rather thin but it's him all right, holding a box of candy canes. There's a tiny person in front of him sucking on a pacifier and wearing a harness and a long leash as though he was a cocker spaniel. I find the situation . . . bittersweet. Two hippies come up, all arrayed in motley and dancing around, ringing bells. Fuck off, says Santa. The tiny starts to cry. Santa walks away. I am outraged. The hippies look astounded. They pick up one end of the leash. This is where we left them. I am shocked as though struck. Fuck off, said Santa Claus.

We also had bad meat in the bottom of a hotel here.

VALDOSTA, GEORGIA

Now this town was very sweet and cool with leaves and trees. We met the governor at a vegetable stand. He is not the governor of this state but of another one. He was buying peanuts and carrots. We are buying endive. Up the road I plan to make a salad and we'll drink Pouilly-Fuissé. It's very European. For example, we've decided to eat from a hamper. The governor says, Well you sure look as though you had a good secret and I wish I had it too.

Well, we say.

Let me give you folks a little something I got right here, the governor says and he hands over a license plate which says ARRIVE ALIVE.

A gimmick, my husband says, a sop!

I agree. I look right into the governor's sunglasses. You're co-old, I say. You're freezzzzing. I must admit I say this girlishly and coy.

Well, the governor says, shaking hands all around. It sure was pleasant meeting you for the first time. He has a beautiful Cadillac car. They leave.

He was certainly a well-put-together man wasn't he, I say. But I don't mean anything by it. I show my husband this by socketing my hip to his. We step back into our crummy Buick and a very judicious thing happens. All hell breaks loose. The car falls apart. I would not speak figuratively. I never do. It falls apart. Its time had come.

A worn battery cable shorted out on the frame, setting fire to the engine at the same time an electrode from the spark plug fell into the combustion chamber, disintegrating the piston. The tires went flat the transmission fluid exploded the gas tank collapsed an armature snapped shooting the generator pulley through the hood the brake shoes melted the windshield cracked and the glove compartment flew open spilling my panties into the street.

My husband is unflustered. A crowd gathers but there's not one dog. I used to have such a way with animals. Dogs don't come near me anymore. I say to him, I think I'm pregnant.

We walk across the street to a car dealer and on the spot he pays in full for the meanest machine I've ever seen.

LAKELAND, FLORIDA

We are at a stoplight, breakfasting hurriedly on gin and orange biscuits. There's a court of appeals in this town. Judges in robes are everywhere, eating barbecue, emerging from hardware stores and so forth. We couldn't care less. He wants only to get somewhere where we can lie down. His collars are too big for him. His cheeks have lovely malignant hollows.

Our car is snarling and burbling at the stoplight. It has air extractors, a shaker hood, six spoilers, four pipes, a 400-cubic-inch Ram Air V-8 and four-barrel carbs. In black and plum.

Of course we're mad for it. I am dying to drive it but I can't push in the clutch. The governor is in the next lane. We destroy him, of course. We stomp the accelerator and five seconds later we are doing sixty. We dust him good.

But I know not forever.

We are in a cozy white cabin on a lake, swinging on a white porch swing. He is asleep but he is loving me up regardless. He is comatose almost always now but he performs beautifully I must say. We talk about sharks. He says he can't understand what he ever had against them. I say, They keep the ocean clean and I thank them for that.

He finds my remarks incisive.

We watch the lake and a fellow and a girl fishing from a little motorboat. They are having a wonderful time but are not catching any fish. Then a big speedboat with a star on it smashes right into them, scattering wood and cushions and hair and sandwiches all over, disrupting the scene to an extent which we would not have thought possible. The girl was a casserole. The fellow went mad. They'd been married only an hour and a half. The deputy sheriff, everyone said thankfully, was unhurt. It could have been a real tragedy. He charged them with having no lifejackets.

We leave immediately for they were innocents and we are as well. Now I have nothing against sheriffs for I am American to the core, but we were innocents, riding and drinking and loving our way to the sea.

KEY WEST, FLORIDA

We are here at Mile 0. I feel sick about it. He is almost gone. We eat lime pie and snapper. The restaurant isn't much. There was a popular restaurant here but it burned down in 1940. We do not look for lodging. I help him down to the beach. All the streets are dead ends naturally. People are selling sponges and shells and baskets made of armadillos, which are always twins, you know. A woman comes up and shouts in his ear, for he has lost most all his faculties. She points out west into the water and screams, Out there was where Dr. Mudd was at. He agrees. I feel that he has given up.

Key West is a pit of salt. And then there is the water. The governor is on the beach surrounded by constituents but his eyes are just on me. I see us reflected in his silver sunglasses. He asks an aide for a Dr. Pepper in a returnable bottle. He gets a Coke in a can.

He is not so hot.

We wade out—to where the green water becomes just blue.

My man, and how can I say I have regrets? tends to me. He moves from desire to object.

So do I. We all do.

Oh! I say. Be mine. And he does. Right where the Gulf of Mexico looks like the Atlantic itself and all around us is seaweed in the shape of little hearts and the sharks are almost where you can see them—swimming and smiling at all the good things there are to do and eat.

That's the advantage of this. For they can't get here too soon.

We kiss.

HEALTH

PAMMY IS IN AN UNPLEASANT TEXAS CITY, THE CITY where she was born, in the month of her twelfth birthday. It is cold and cloudy. Soon it will rain. The rain will wash the film of ash off the car she is traveling in, volcanic ash that has drifted across the Gulf of Mexico, all the way from the Yucatán. Pammy is a stocky gray-eyed blonde, a daughter, traveling in her father's car, being taken to her tanning lesson.

This is her father's joke. She is being taken to a tanning session, twenty-five minutes long. She had requested this for her birthday, ten tanning sessions in a health spa. She had also asked for and received new wheels for her skates. They are purple Rannalli's. She had dyed her stoppers to match although the match was not perfect. The stoppers were a duller, cruder purple. Pammy wants to be a speed skater but she worries that she doesn't have the personality for it. "You've gotta have gravel

111

in your gut to be in speed," her coach said. Pammy has mastered the duck walk but still doesn't have a good, smooth crossover, and sometimes she fears that she never will.

Pammy and her father, Morris, are following a truck which is carrying a jumble of television sets. There is a twenty-four-inch console facing them on the open tailgate, restrained by rope, with a bullet hole in the exact center of the screen.

Morris drinks coffee from a plastic-lidded cup that fits into a bracket mounted just beneath the car's radio. Pammy has a friend, Wanda, whose stepfather has the same kind of plastic cup in his car, but he drinks bourbon and water from his. Wanda had been adopted when she was two months old. Pammy is relieved that neither her father nor Marge, her mother, drinks. Sometimes they have wine. On her birthday, even Pammy had wine with dinner. Marge and Morris seldom quarrel and she is grateful for this. This morning, however, she had seen them quarrel. Once again, her mother had borrowed her father's hairbrush and left long, brown hairs in it. Her father had taken the brush and cleaned it with a comb over the clean kitchen sink. Her father had left a nest of brown hair in the white sink.

In the car, the radio is playing a song called "Tainted Love," a song Morris likes to refer to as "Rancid Love." The radio plays constantly when Pammy and her father drive anywhere. Morris is a good driver. He is fast and doesn't bear grudges. He enjoys driving still, after years and years of it. Pammy looks forward to learning how to drive now, but after a few years, who knows? She can't imagine it being that enjoyable after a while. Her father is skillful here, on the freeways and streets, and on the terrifying, wide two-lane highways and narrow mountain roads in Mexico, and even on the rutted, soiled beaches of the Gulf Coast. One weekend, earlier that spring,

Morris had rented a Jeep in Corpus Christi and he and Pammy and Marge had driven the length of Padre Island. They sped across the sand, the only people for miles and miles. There was plastic everywhere.

"You will see a lot of plastic," the man who rented them the Jeep said, "but it is plastic from all over the world."

Morris had given Pammy a lesson in driving the Jeep. He taught her how to shift smoothly, how to synchronize acceleration with the depression and release of the clutch. "There's a way to do things right," Morris told her and when he said this she was filled with a sort of fear. They were just words, she knew, words that anybody could use, but behind words were always things, sometimes things you could never tell anyone, certainly no one you loved, frightening things that weren't even true.

"I'm sick of being behind this truck," Morris says. The screen of the injured television looks like dirty water. Morris pulls to the curb beside an Oriental market. Pammy stares into the market where shoppers wait in line at a cash register. Many of the women wear scarves on their heads. Pammy is deeply disturbed by Orientals who kill penguins to make gloves and murder whales to make nail polish. In school, in social studies class, she is reading eyewitness accounts of the aftermath of the atomic bombing of Hiroshima. She reads about young girls running from their melting city, their hair burnt off, their burnt skin in loose folds, crying, "Stupid Americans." Morris sips his coffee, then turns the car back onto the street, a street now free from fatally wounded television sets.

Pammy gazes at the backs of her hands which are tan, but, she feels, not tan enough. They are a dusky peach color. This will be her fifth tanning lesson. In the health spa, there are ten colored photographs on the wall showing a woman in a bikini, a pale woman being transformed into a tanned woman. In the last photograph she has plucked the bikini slightly away from her hipbone to expose a sliver of white skin and she is smiling down at the sliver.

Pammy tans well. Without a tan, her face seems grainy and uneven for she has freckles and rather large pores. Tanning draws her together, completes her. She has had all kinds of tans—golden tans, pool tans, even a Florida tan which seemed yellow back in Texas. She had brought all her friends the same present from Florida—small plywood crates filled with tiny oranges which were actually chewing gum. The finest tan Pammy has ever had, however, was in Mexico six months ago. She had gone there with her parents for two weeks, and she had gotten a truly remarkable tan and she had gotten tuberculosis. This has caused some tension between Morris and Marge as it had been Morris's idea to swim at the spas in the mountains rather than in the pools at the more established hotels. It was believed that Pammy had become infected at one particular public spa just outside the small dusty town where they had gone to buy tiles, tiles of a dusky orange with blue rays flowing from the center, tiles which are now in the kitchen of their home where each morning Pammy drinks her juice and takes three hundred milligrams of isoniazid.

"Here we are," Morris says. The health spa is in a small, concrete block building with white columns, salvaged from the wrecking of a mansion, adorning the front. There are gift shops, palmists and all-night restaurants along the street, as well as an exterminating company that has a huge fiberglass bug with Xs for eyes on the roof. This was not the company that had tented Wanda's house for termites. That had been another company. When Pammy was in Mexico getting tuberculosis, Wanda and her parents had gone to San Antonio for a week while their house was being tented. When they returned, they'd found a dead robber in the living room, the things he was stealing piled neatly nearby. He had died from inhaling the deadly gas used by the exterminators.

"Mommy will pick you up," Morris says. "She has a class this afternoon so she might be a little late. Just stay inside until she comes."

Morris kisses her on the cheek. He treats her like a child. He treats Marge like a mother, her mother.

Marge is thirty-five but she is still a student. She takes courses in art history and film at one of the city's universities, the same university where Morris teaches petroleum science. Years ago when Marge had first been a student, before she had met Morris and Pammy had been born, she had been in Spain, in a museum studying a Goya and a piece of the painting had fallen at her feet. She had quickly placed it in her pocket and now has it on her bureau in a small glass box. It is a wedge of greenish-violet paint, as large as a thumbnail. It is from one of Goya's nudes.

Pammy gets out of the car and goes into the health spa. There is no equipment here except for the tanning beds, twelve tanning beds in eight small rooms. Pammy has never had to share a room with anyone. If asked to, she would probably say no, hoping that she would not hurt the other person's feelings. The receptionist is an old, vigorous woman behind a scratched metal desk, wearing a black jumpsuit and feather earrings. Behind her are shelves of powders and pills in squat brown bottles with names like DYNAMIC STAMINA BUILDER and DYNAMIC SUPER STRESS–END and LIVER CONCENTRATE ENERGIZER.

The receptionist's name is Aurora. Pammy thinks that the name is magnificent and is surprised that it belongs to such an old woman. Aurora leads her to one of the rooms at the rear of the building. The room has a mirror, a sink, a small stool, a white rotating fan and the bed, a long bronze coffinlike apparatus with a lid. Pammy is always startled when she sees the bed with its frosted ultraviolet tubes, its black vinyl headrest. In the next room, someone coughs. Pammy imagines people lying in all the rooms, wrapped in white light, lying quietly as though they were being rested for a long, long journey. Aurora takes a spray bottle of disinfectant and a scrap of toweling from the counter above the sink and cleans the surface of the bed. She twists the timer and the light leaps out, like an animal in a dream, like a murderer in a movie.

"There you are, honey," Aurora says. She pats Pammy on the shoulder and leaves.

Pammy pushes off her sandals and undresses quickly. She leaves her clothes in a heap, her sweatshirt on top of the pile. Her sweatshirt is white with a transfer of a skater on the back. The skater is a man wearing a helmet and kneepads, side-surfing goofy-footed. She lies down and with her left hand pulls the lid to within a foot of the bed's cool surface. She can see the closed door and the heap of clothing and her feet. Pammy considers her feet to be her ugliest feature. They are skinny and the toes are too far apart. She and Wanda had painted their toes the same color, but Wanda's feet were pretty and hers were not. Pammy thought her feet looked like they belonged to a dead person and there wasn't anything she could do about them. She closes her eyes.

Wanda, who read a lot, told Pammy that tuberculosis was a very romantic disease, the disease of artists and poets and "highly sensitive individuals."

"Oh yeah," her stepfather had said. "Tuberculosis has mucho cachet."

Wanda's stepfather speaks loudly and his eyes glitter. He is always joking, Pammy thinks. Pammy feels that Wanda's parents are pleasant but she's always a little uncomfortable around them. Wanda wasn't the first child they had adopted. There had been another baby, but it was learned that the baby's background had been misrepresented. Or perhaps it had been a boring baby. In any case the baby had been returned and they got Wanda. Pammy doesn't think Wanda's parents are very steadfast. She is surprised that they don't make Wanda nervous.

The tanning bed is warm but not uncomfortably so. Pammy lies with her arms straight by her sides, palms down. She hears voices in the hall and footsteps. When she first began coming to the health spa, she was afraid that someone would open the door to the room she was in by mistake. She imagined exactly what it would be like. She would see the door open abruptly out of the corner of her eye, then someone would say, "Sorry," and the door would close again. But this had not happened. The voices pass by.

Pammy thinks of Snow White lying in her glass coffin. The queen had deceived her how many times? Three? She had been in disguise, but still. And then Snow White had choked on an apple. In the restaurants she sometimes goes to with her parents there are posters on the walls which show a person choking and another person trying to save him. The posters take away Pammy's appetite.

Snow White lay in a glass coffin, not naked of course but in a gown, watched over by dwarfs. But surely they had not been real dwarfs. That had just been a word that had been given to them.

When Pammy had told Morris that tuberculosis was a romantic disease, he had said, "There's nothing romantic about it. Besides, you don't have it."

It seems to be a fact that she both has and doesn't have tuberculosis. Pammy had been given the tuberculin skin test along with her classmates when she began school in the fall and within forty-eight hours had a large swelling on her arm.

"Now that you've come in contact with it, you don't have to worry about getting it," the pediatrician had said in his office, smiling.

"You mean the infection constitutes immunity," Marge said.

"Not exactly," the pediatrician said, shaking his head, still smiling.

Her lungs are clear. She is not ill but has an illness. The germs are in her body, but in a resting state, still alive but rendered powerless, successfully overcome by her healthy body's strong defenses. Outwardly, she is the same, but within, a great drama had taken place and Pammy feels herself in possession of a bright, secret, and unspeakable knowledge.

She knows other things too, things that would break her parents' hearts, common, ugly, easy things. She knows a girl in school who stole her mother's Green Stamps and bought a personal massager with the books. She knows another girl whose brother likes to wear her clothes. She knows a boy who threw a can of motor oil at his father and knocked him unconscious.

Pammy stretches. Her head tingles. Her body is about a foot and a half off the floor and appears almost gray in the glare from the tubes. She has heard of pills one could take to acquire a tan. One just took two pills a day and after twenty days one had a wonderful tan which could be maintained by continuing to take the pills. You ordered them from Canada. It was some kind of food-coloring substance. How gross, Pammy thinks. When she had been little she had bought a quarter of an acre of land in Canada by mail for fifty cents. That had been two years ago.

Pammy hears voices from the room next to hers, coming

through the thin wall. A woman talking rapidly says, "Pete went up to Detroit two days ago to visit his brother who's dying up there in the hospital. Cancer. The brother's always been a nasty type, I mean very unpleasant. Younger than Pete and always mean. Tried to commit suicide twice. Then he learns he has cancer and decides he doesn't want to die. Carries on and on. Is miserable to everyone. Puts the whole family through hell, but nothing can be done about it, he's dying of cancer. So Pete goes up to see him his last days in the hospital and you know what happens? Pete's wallet gets stolen. Right out of a dying man's room. Five hundred dollars in cash and all our credit cards. That was yesterday. What a day."

Another woman says, "If it's not one thing, it's something else."

Pammy coughs. She doesn't want to hear other people's voices. It is as though they are throwing away junk, the way some people use words, as though one word were as good as another.

"Things happen so abruptly anymore," the woman says. "You know what I mean?"

Pammy does not listen and she does not open her eyes for if she did she would see this odd bright room with her clothes in a heap and herself lying motionless and naked. She does not open her eyes because she prefers imagining that she is a magician's accomplice, levitating on a stage in a coil of pure energy. If one thought purely enough, one could create one's own truth. That's how people accomplished astral travel, walked over burning coals, cured warts. There was a girl in Pammy's class at school, Bonnie Black, a small owlish looking girl who was a Christian Scientist. She raised rabbits and showed them at fairs, and was always wearing the ribbons they had won to school, pinned to her blouse. She had warts all over her hands, but one day Pammy noticed that the warts were gone and Bonnie Black had told her that the warts disappeared after she had clearly realized that in her true being as God's reflection, she couldn't have warts.

It seemed that people were better off when they could concentrate on something, hold something in their mind for a long time and really believe it. Pammy had once seen a radical skater putting on a show at the opening of a shopping mall. He leapt over cars and pumped up the sides of buildings. He did flips and spins. A disc jockey who was set up for the day in the parking lot interviewed him. "I'm really impressed with your performance," the disc jockey said, "and I'm impressed that you never fall. Why don't you fall?" The skater was a thin boy in baggy cutoff jeans. "I don't fall," the boy said, looking hard at the microphone, "because I've got a deep respect for the concrete surface and because when I make a miscalculation, instead of falling, I turn it into a new trick."

Pammy thinks it is wonderful that the boy was able to say something which would keep him from thinking he might fall.

The door to the room opened. Pammy had heard the turning of the knob. At first she lies without opening her eyes, willing the sound of the door shutting, but she hears nothing, only the ticking of the bed's timer. She swings her head quickly to the side and looks at the door. There is a man standing there, staring at her. She presses her right hand into a fist and lays it between her legs. She puts her left arm across her breasts.

"What?" she says to the figure, frightened. In an instant she is almost panting with fear. She feels the repetition of something painful and known, but she has not known this, not ever. The figure says nothing and pulls the door shut. With a flurry of rapid ticking, the timer stops. The harsh lights of the bed go out.

Pammy pushes the lid back and hurriedly gets up. She dresses hastily and smooths her hair with her fingers. She looks at herself in the mirror, her lips parted. Her teeth are white behind her pale lips. She stares at herself. She can be looked at and not discovered. She can speak and not be known. She opens the door and enters the hall. There is no one there. The hall is so narrow that by spreading her arms she can touch the walls with her fingertips. In the reception area by Aurora's desk, there are three people, a stoop-shouldered young woman and two men. The woman was signing up for a month of unlimited tanning which meant that after the basic monthly fee she only had to pay a dollar a visit. She takes her checkbook out of a soiled handbag, which is made out of some silvery material, and writes a check. The men look comfortable lounging in the chairs, their legs stretched out. They know one another, Pammy guesses, but they do not know the woman. One of them has dark spikey hair like a wet animal's. The other wears a red tight T-shirt. Neither is the man she had seen in the doorway.

"What time do you want to come back tomorrow, honey?" Aurora asks Pammy. "You certainly are coming along nicely. Isn't she coming along nicely?"

"I'd like to come back the same time tomorrow," Pammy says. She raises her hand to her mouth and coughs slightly.

"Not the same time, honey. Can't give you the same time. How about an hour later?"

"All right," Pammy says. The stoop-shouldered woman sits down in a chair. There are no more chairs in the room. Pammy opens the door and steps outside. It has rained and the street is dark and shining. She walks slowly down the street and smells the rain lingering in the trees. By a store called Imagine, there's a clump of bamboo with some beer cans glittering in its ragged, grassy center. Imagine sells neon palm trees and silk clouds and stars. It sells greeting cards and chocolate in shapes children aren't allowed to see and it sells children stickers and shoelaces.

Pammy looks in the window at a satin pillow in the shape of a heart with a heavy zipper running down the center of it. Pammy turns and walks back to the building that houses the tanning beds. Her mother pulls up in their car. "Pammy!" she calls. She is leaning toward the window on the passenger side which she has rolled down. She unlocks the car's door. Pammy gets in and the door locks again.

The car speeds down the street and Pammy sits in it, a little stunned. Her father will teach her how to drive, and she will drive around. Her mother will continue to take classes at the university. Whenever she meets someone new, she will mention the Goya. "I have a small Goya," she will say, and laugh. Pammy will grow older, she is older now. But the world will remain as young as she was once, infinite in its possibilities, and uncaring. She never wants to see that figure looking at her again, so coldly staring, but she knows she will, for already its features are becoming more indistinct, more general. It could be anything. And it will be somewhere else now, something else. She coughs, but it is not the cough of a sick person because Pammy is a healthy girl. It is the kind of cough a person might make if they were at a party and there was no one there but strangers.

WHITE

BLISS AND JOAN WERE GIVING A FAREWELL PARTY
for the Episcopal priest and his family who had been called by
God to the state of Michigan. They had invited some mutual
friends and couples with children the same age as the priest's
children. Bliss did not go to church and had never met the
priest, but he approved of any party given for whatever reason
and he felt that Joan had something of a fascination with the
man, whose name was Daniel. Joan had always imagined that
Daniel might tell her something, although he never had, and
now he was leaving.

This was in New England where they had lived for three
years. Joan was a fourth-generation Floridian who missed the
garish sunsets and the sound of armadillos crashing through the
palmetto scrub. As a child, she remembered wearing live lizards
hanging from her earlobes. She remembered a pony her father

123

had bought for her named "Gator." Joan's father owned a grapefruit grove. Her grandfather had run a fishing camp, and her great-grandfather had been a guide who shot flamingos and spoonbills and ibis and gathered eggs for naturalists.

Bliss had been born in Florida too. Now he's a dentist. People think that dentists are acquisitive and don't care, but Bliss cares.

Bliss and Joan have no children. Twice, Joan gave birth to a baby but both times the baby died before he was six months old. There was a sweet smell on the baby's diaper, a smell rather like that of maple sugar, and in a few hours, the baby was dead. Bliss has a single deviant gene that matches a single deviant gene of Joan's. When a doctor told him at the hospital that the deaths were not as mysterious as they first appeared to be, Bliss struck him before he could say anything more, once with his left hand and once with his right. The doctor fell to the floor but got up quickly and walked away, down the white corridor, leaving Bliss alone, his arms aching.

After the death of their second child, they had moved to New England. In Florida, Joan's depression had been compounded by unpleasant dreams of her great-grandfather. He appeared in her dreams exactly as he did in her father's photo album—a skinny man in a wide hat, rough clothes and rubber boots, standing with his shotgun. In a recurrent dream, he was a waiter in a pleasant, rosily lit dining room serving her soup in which birds in all stages of incubation floated. In another, frequent dream, he was not visible, yet Joan sensed his presence beneath the vision of hundreds of flamingos flying through a dark sky, flying, as they do, in a serpentine manner, as though they were crawling through the air.

In New England, Joan discovered that if she slept while it

was light she didn't dream, so she slept in the afternoons and stayed up all night, cooking meals for the days ahead and putting together immense puzzles of Long Island Sound. She lived in terror, actually, but it was rootless, because the worst had already happened. She referred to the days behind her as "those so-called days."

The day of the party was a Saturday, and Bliss had shopped with Joan for the liquor and food. As they were turning into their driveway, their car was struck in the rear by a woman in an old Triumph convertible with a hard top. Joan and Bliss got out and looked at the rear of their car, which was undamaged, and then at the Triumph, which appeared undamaged also.

The woman was weeping. "I'm sorry," she wailed, "oh, I'm so sorry. This is my husband's car."

"No harm done," Bliss said.

The woman tore at her hair. She was pale and her hair was dark. She was very pretty.

Joan was unaffected by trivial unpleasantries and looked at the woman impatiently. Then she got back into the car and drove to the house, while Bliss remained standing by the Triumph. Joan unloaded the car and then went outside with a large bag of Hershey kisses. She hid the kisses all around the lawn, in the interstices of the stone walls and on the lower branches of trees for the children at the party to find.

"Well, Donna certainly has a tale to tell," Bliss said, coming up to her. He unwrapped the foil from a kiss and tossed the chocolate into his mouth.

"Donna, the TR person," Joan said.

"I invited her to the party. Is that all right?"

"Sure," Joan said. Bliss often invited strangers to their parties. Sometimes they were very nice people.

"Her husband had a stroke and is divorcing her. He insists upon it." Bliss rolled the foil into a tiny ball, looked at it, then dropped it in his pocket.

"We won't get divorced," Joan said.

"Never," Bliss said. He went into the house to set out the glasses and plates. Joan walked around outside, hiding the rest of the candy. In the yard next door was a Doberman with bandages on his ears and tail, playing with a rubber ice-cream sundae. His aluminum run extended the length of the yard. He had a druggy name, the name of some amphetamine. Joan had heard his owner calling him. The owner was a muscular man with a mustache who drove an elaborate four-wheel-drive vehicle. The puppy's fashionable name made him seem transitory, even doomed.

At five P.M., Joan and Bliss went upstairs to their bedroom. The room was simple and pleasant with plain wideboard floors and white furniture, a little cell of felicity. There was a single framed poster of wildflowers on the white walls. It seemed to Joan the kind of room in which someone was supposed to be getting better. Joan lay on the bed and watched Bliss change his clothes for the party. She smiled for an instant, then shut her eyes. The passion they felt for one another had turned to fear some time ago.

"Maybe you'd love me if I were a priest," Bliss said.

Joan's eyes were shut. She saw the green lawn below them extending in time to her parents' house, herself as the child her own children would never remind her of. She saw the barn where her father kept the chemicals and sprays for the groves. Inside, tacked on one wall, was a large foldout from an insecticide manufacturer's brochure depicting all the ills that citrus was heir to. Beneath each picture of an insect was a picture of the horrible damage it could do. As a child, she had thrilled to it,

126

flyspecked, yellowing, curling around the rusted nails that secured it. That such cruel and destructive forces could exist and be named amazed her, that the means to control them could be at hand seemed preposterous. She saw it often, as now, clearly; the meticulous detail, the particularity of each proffered blight.

"It's a question of language," Bliss said. " 'The periapical granuloma is one of the most common of all sequelae of pulpitis'—it's not the kind of language that sends a person forth into the world feeling loved, forgiven and renewed."

"It's not very comforting," Joan agreed.

"Really," Bliss said, "I'm sick of teeth. You wouldn't believe what goes on in people's mouths. I want to abandon dentistry and go into the ministry."

"What about your patients?" Joan said, laughing. She had a sweet, startling laugh.

"They're hopeless," Bliss said.

Joan pushed a pillow up against the headboard and opened her eyes. She saw a handsome man in brick-red trousers pulling a white shirt from the bureau drawer.

"Do you know something?" she asked. "Would you share it if you did?"

"I have already chosen my style," Bliss said, addressing her face in the mirror. "Yesterday when Peter Carlyle was in— he's the acute suppurative osteomyelitis—I said, 'This day only is ours for the life of a man comes upon him slowly and insensibly.' "

"Did he agree?"

"He certainly did," Bliss said. "That is, he nodded slightly and groaned. Would you like a drink?"

"Sure," Joan said. "It's a party."

Bliss went downstairs and reappeared a few moments later with a glass of bourbon and ice. Joan ran a bath and sat in the tub and drank the bourbon, listening to the cars coming up the driveway, the slamming of doors and people's greetings. She thought about Daniel, his voice, his prematurely gray hair. He had big feet. The shoes he wore in church seemed enormous. Joan went to church several times a week and sat, rose or knelt in accordance with the service. She sat in the back, in a pew where someone had once outlined a flower in the brocade of the kneeling bench with green crayon. In each pew, by the hymnal rack, was a smaller rack holding printed information cards and a small sharpened pencil. One could introduce oneself, ask questions, request a hymn, seek counseling. Joan did none of these things. She sat quietly in church, her head tilted upward, listening, feeling vain, unfixed, distracted. With Daniel she felt she was close to something, some comprehension of what there was left for her to want. Bliss was right, she thought, to be jealous of Daniel, although she and the priest were little more than acquaintances. And Daniel, of course, doesn't know anything about her—he doesn't know the past, about the babies, he doesn't know her breasts, her lips. He doesn't know the terrible way she thinks, like Bliss knows.

Joan got out of the tub. She was thin and tanned. Wide veins were darkly visible on her hands and feet. She painted her nails chalk-colored, put on a flowered dress and went down to the party on the lawn. There were several dozen adults there and half a dozen children. The children were sitting meditatively in a circle. Joan approached them slowly, wondering what was in the heart of the circle, a baby bird? a Ouija board? but saw from a distance that it was a bowl of potato chips. The sky was pale and the ragged crown of the trees, dark. She gazed at the children without really seeing them. If someone had demanded that she describe them, she could not. She yawned. She and Bliss gave a great many parties and were reciprocally invited to many. There was nothing to it, really.

A man named Tim Barnes came up to her and kissed her cheek. Tim liked to sail. He enjoyed tight rivers and winding estuaries. He had fashioned a story around the time his mast went through the branches of a tree, and often he would tell it. When he told it, he would say, "I proceeded, looking like Birnam Wood."

Once, during another party, Tim had said to Joan. "I dream about you, and when I wake up, I'm angry. What do you think?"

People were talking and laughing. Joan had a tendency to look at their mouths. Their teeth seemed good. Bliss had made the acquaintance of many of these people professionally. She imagined Bliss solving their mouths, making them attractive, happy, her friends.

Next door, the Doberman trotted back and forth the length of his run, watching them. He had an abrupt, rocking gait. His paws, striking the soft dirt, made no sound.

Joan poured herself a drink, picked a sprig of mint from a bowl beside the bottles, crushed it and dropped it into her glass.

People were talking about whether or not they wanted to survive a nuclear war.

"I certainly wouldn't," Tim Barnes's wife said.

"I don't believe we're talking about nuclear war just like our parents did in the fifties," a woman named Petey said.

Joan saw a clutch of candy at the base of a slender crabapple tree. She should have hidden something less bright. She had to remember to tell the children that they were supposed to look for the candy. She thought of her father spraying water on his citrus before a freeze. The next morning, the globes of fruit would be white and shining and rotting in the clear sunny air. Florida was not a serious state.

"The first thing our government is going to do after the Big B is to implement their post-attack taxation plan," Tim Barnes said.

"I mean," his wife said, "who wants to survive only to pay forty or fifty percent?"

"You have to protect the banking system," Tim said. "You have to reestablish the productive base."

"I have to greet the guest of honor," Joan said. The group, for the most part, chuckled. Joan walked toward Daniel, who was standing at the bottom of the lawn. He had a drink in one hand and a pretzel rod in the other and was gazing into a bed of delphiniums. Several yards away, Donna, the TR person, was talking to Bliss.

"People need dentists," Joan heard her assure him, "they really do."

"Joan!" Daniel exclaimed as she drew near, "what a beautiful garden." He wore a green shirt and a poplin suit. His large feet were encased in sneakers. "Cast completely in blue and white. Very discriminating, very elegant. It must have been difficult."

Joan looked at her garden which gave her no pleasure. She had designed it and cared for it. She knew some things. It didn't matter.

"White is a distinctively modern color," Daniel said, finishing his drink. "It takes the curse off things."

"Its neutrality is its charm," Joan said.

The priest sighed. "I want to clarify what I just said, Joan. You can't imagine how tired I am. Claire was so tired, she couldn't make it. The hustle-bustle of moving is exhausting. She's going to write you a note. You will definitely receive a note from her. I meant, and this is not in regard to your garden, which is stunning, that white is often used to make otherwise unacceptable things acceptable. In general."

"Some people feel that flowers are in bad taste," Joan said.

"Isn't that astounding," Daniel said. "Someone told me that once in regard to the altar and I found it astounding." He rolled his empty glass between his hands and nodded toward the puppy, who was resting on his haunches now, regarding the group in the dimming light.

"Your cats must be afraid of that Doberman," he said.

"I don't have cats."

"I'm sorry, I thought you had two cats. Perhaps it's Joan Pillsbury who has two cats."

One of Daniel's sons came up to them and said, "Can I watch TV, Dad?" Daniel looked at him. Joan told the boy about the hidden candy and in a moment the small group of children had scattered across the yard with shrill cries. An instant later, they had found it all and returned to the small piece of earth that they had appropriated for themselves. They displayed the amount, then ate it.

"That was fun," the priest said. "They all certainly enjoyed that."

"Dentists talk a lot, don't they," Donna said to Bliss. "I mean, I've always wondered, why are dentists so garrulous?"

"Look," Bliss said, "my wife has turned on the moon." The two couples had drifted together and now looked upward at a full, close, mauve moon.

"My wife fell from that tree once, you know," Bliss said, addressing Daniel, pointing toward a large maple.

"You didn't," the priest said to Joan. He shook his head.

"Uh-huh," Bliss said. "Several years ago."

"How did it happen?" Daniel said, weaving his eyes among the branches, down the trunk to the ground beneath it as though he expected to see her splayed form there, outlined in lime by some secular authority. "Was one of your cats up there with his eye on the sparrow?" He chuckled.

"I would have broken my neck," Donna said. She laughed but her eyes were wet. Her mouth trembled a little.

"Nothing happened," Joan said. "Here I am."

"I understand what you're saying, Joan," Daniel said. "You took a little rest but now you're back among us."

Donna looked at the priest and then at Joan.

"Make yourself another drink," Bliss said to the priest. "We don't stand on ceremony here."

"May I make for anyone?" Daniel asked.

"I believe you married us," Donna said to Daniel. "St. Steven's, right? Harry and Donna Sutton?"

"Hello," Daniel said warmly.

"We weren't members. You just fit us in."

There was a pause while they all sipped their fresh drinks.

"Do you know that at any given moment there are approximately five hundred and eighty-four million unfilled carious lesions in the teeth of the U.S. population?" Bliss said.

Donna laughed, then turned and walked unsteadily to one of the long stone benches on the lawn. She put her drink down on the grass, then lay on the bench. She crossed her ankles.

"You'd like Donna," Bliss said to Joan. "You know where she's from? Panama City."

"How are she and Harry doing?" Daniel asked. "He was considerably older than she if I recall."

"Time has wrought its meanness on their attachment," Bliss said. "You know what I told her? I told her, to God both the day and the night are alike, so are the first and last of our days."

"My, that's very good," Daniel said, "but a bit cold."

"I told her sufficient to the day is the evil thereof."

"One of the great lines, certainly."

"Are you of the school that thinks of man as a vapor, a fantastic vapor, or a shadow, even the dream of a shadow?" Bliss asked.

"Stop," Joan said. She stifled a yawn because she wanted to appear rude.

"A bubble," Daniel said. "We subscribe to the bubble theory."

"Excuse me, Father," Bliss said. "I'm sure this happens to you all the time, people asking you questions on an emergency basis at cocktail parties."

Daniel stretched his tanned neck and smiled at Joan.

Bliss took several swallows of his drink. "An interesting thing happened today," he said. "Joan's father sent us a letter. It began briskly enough. 'Dear Joan and Bliss' it began. But then there was nothing, not a thing. Just a page, blank as the day is long. Well, we puzzled over that one, you can imagine."

"Faith illuminates that letter for us," Daniel said. "Love is the great translator. On the other hand, how's Dad's eyesight? Does he buy good-quality pens or does he buy them twenty for ninety-nine cents?"

"The man refuses to be a guest," Bliss laughed. "Actually, I don't know why I made that up about the letter."

"I'm a little giddy tonight myself," Daniel said. "I suppose it's the thrill of saddling up and moving on."

Bliss put his hand on Joan's back and lightly touched her hair. For an instant Joan hated him, and in another instant felt sick, drowning. She saw the party set up beneath the trees, illuminated by candles stuck in paper bags of sand. People were eating ribs and salad from large china plates. Donna remained lying on her back on the bench, her arms dangling, her hands, loosely curved, touching the grass. Joan pulled away from Bliss and walked over to her. The girl's eyes were open and she wore shiny pants, pegged and zippered at the ankles. Her blouse looped out over her belt.

"Can I get you something to eat?" Joan asked. She was

solicitous and incurious. But people were supposed to be making connections like these, she thought, all the time, all through their lives.

The girl sat up abruptly. "I shouldn't be behaving like this, should I? I'm making a fool of myself, aren't I?" Joan sat beside her on the bench. "My husband's sick and doesn't want me any more," Donna said. "When he was well he was always saying he didn't want me to have a baby yet. He said he wanted to wait awhile before we had a baby. Men always act as though the same baby is waiting out there in the dark each month, do you ever notice that?"

At the edge of the party, Amanda Sherrill, her long peach-colored hair shining and swinging, demonstrated a hip-slimming exercise to a small exuberant group. She grasped the seat of a lawn chair and extended her left leg upward in a slow arc.

"Oh my goodness," Jack Buttrick screamed.

"Your husband is very pleasant," Donna said. "He's funny, isn't he? And you're pleasant. It was very nice of you to invite me here. I'd been driving around all day in Harry's car, just driving and crying to myself and then I hit you. You were so nice about it." She looked at Joan uneasily. "Your husband thinks we're a little alike," she said. "I never would have guessed you were from the South. Do you miss Florida?"

"My father always used to call it Floridon't," Joan said. This was the way it was supposed to be, she thought. Memory and conversation, clarification and semblance, miscalculation and repentance, skim and rest.

Donna laughed, showing considerable gum. Bliss isn't going to be able to do much about that, Joan thought. "I'll get us something to eat," she said. She walked toward the house, having no intention of getting anyone anything to eat. The children were in the darkened living room, watching a small television screen. In the kitchen, one man was saying to another, "The secret to hamburgers is ice in the patty before broiling. That's the secret."

Joan went up to the second floor, entered the bedroom and closed the door. She stood by the window and looked down into the adjoining yard. The muscular young man with the mustache had gone into the pen and was playing with the Doberman. The dog spun in tight, exhilarated circles. The man put his hands on the dog's shoulders and pushed him from side to side. Joan stood by the window, watching. Moonlight pushed into the room and across the ribbon of earth where the man and the dog lovingly pulled and turned and rose against one another. Then the man grasped the dog by the collar and led him into the house and the pen was empty.

Some time later, Bliss came into the room. He stood behind her and put his arms around her. His face was damp and his hair smelled of cigarette smoke.

"Do you remember when we drove up here," Joan said, "when it was finished?"

"Don't whisper," Bliss said.

"We left everything behind and we drove all through the night and in the morning we stopped at this little picnic grove by a river and there were two old people there and they were washing this big white dog in the river. A big old white dog. They washed him so carefully and then they dried him with a towel. He was what they had."

"Everyone's about to leave," Bliss said. "Let's go down and say good-night."

"I don't want to be like those old people," Joan said.

"Never," Bliss said. "Let's go down and say good-night. Just this one more time."

THE BLUE MEN

❦

BOMBER BOYD, AGE THIRTEEN, TOLD HIS NEW AC-
quaintances that summer that his father had been executed by
the state of Florida for the murder of a sheriff's deputy and his
drug-sniffing German shepherd.

"It's a bummer he killed the dog," a girl said.

"Guns, chair, or lethal injection?" a boy asked.

"Chair," Bomber said. He was sorry he had mentioned the
dog in the same breath. The dog had definitely not been necessary.

"Lethal injection is fascist, man; who does lethal injection?"
a small, fierce-looking boy said.

"Florida, Florida, Florida," the girl murmured. "We went
to Key West once. We did sunset. We did Sloppy's. We bought
conch-shell lamps with tiny plastic flamingos and palm trees
inside lit up by tiny lights." The girl's hair was cut in a high

Mohawk that rose at least half a foot in the air. She was pale, her skin flawless except for one pimple artfully flourishing above her full upper lip.

"Key West isn't Florida," a boy said.

There were six of them standing around, four boys and two girls. Bomber stood there with them, waiting.

❧

May was in her garden looking through a stack of a hundred photographs that her son and daughter-in-law had taken years before when they had visited Morocco. Bomber had been four at the time and May had taken care of him all that spring. There were pictures of camels, walled towns, tiled staircases, and large vats of colored dyes on rooftops. May turned the pictures methodically. There were men washing their heads in a marble ablutions basin. On a dusty road there was the largest pile of carrots May had ever seen. May had been through the photographs many many times. She slowly approached the one that never ceased to trouble her, a picture of her child in the city of Fez. He wore khaki pants and a polo shirt and was squatting beside a blanket upon which teeth were arranged. It had been explained to May that there were many self-styled dentists in Morocco who pulled teeth and then arranged them on plates and sold them. In the photograph, her son looked healthy, muscular, and curious, but there was something unfamiliar about his face. It had begun there, May thought, somehow. She put the photographs down and picked up a collection of post-cards from that time, most of them addressed to Bomber. May held one close to her eyes. Men in blue burnouses lounged against their camels, the desert wilderness behind them. On the back was written, *The blue men! We wanted so much to see them but we never did.*

❧

    May and Bomber were trying out their life together in a new town. They had only each other, for Bomber's mother was resting in California, where she would probably be resting for quite some time, and May's husband Harold was dead. In the new town, which was on an island, May had bought a house and planted a pretty little flower garden. She had two big rooms upstairs that she rented out by the week to tourists. One was in yellow and one was in gray. May liked to listen to the voices in the rooms, but as a rule her tourists didn't say much. Actually, she strained to hear at times. She was not listening for sounds of love, of course. The sounds of love were not what mattered, after all.

    Once, as she was standing in the upstairs hallway, polishing a small table there, her husband's last words had returned to her. Whether they had been spoken again by someone in the room, either in the gray room or the yellow room, she did not quite know, but there they were. *That doctor is so stuck on himself* . . . the same words as Harold's very last ones.

    The tourists would gather seashells and then leave them behind when they left. They left them on the bureaus and on the windowsills and May would pick them up and take them back to the beach. At night when she could not sleep she would walk downtown to a bar where the young people danced called the Lucky Kittens and have a glass of beer. The Lucky Kittens was a loud and careless place where there was dancing all night long. May sat alone at a table near the door, an old lady, dignified and out of place.

❧

Bomber was down at the dock, watching tourists arrive on the ferry. The tourists were grinning, and ready for anything, they thought. Two boys were playing catch with a tennis ball on the pier, a young boy and an older one in a college sweatshirt. The younger one sidled back and forth close to the pier's edge, catching in both hands the high, lobbed throws the other boy threw. The water was high and dark and flecked with oil and they were both laughing like lunatics. Bomber believed they were brothers and he enjoyed watching them.

A girl moved languidly across the dock toward him. She was the pale girl with the perfect pimple and she touched it delicately as she walked. Her shaved temples had a slight sheen of baby powder on them. Her name was Edith.

"I've been thinking," Edith said, "and I think that what they should do, like, a gesture is enough. Like for murderers they could make them wear black all the time. They could walk around but they'd have to be always in black and they'd have to wear a mask of some sort."

Sometimes Bomber thought of what had happened to his father as an operation. It was an operation they had performed. "A mask," he said. "Hey." He crossed his arms tight across his chest. He thought Edith's long, pale face beautiful.

She nodded. "A mask," she said. "Something really amazing."

"But that wouldn't be enough, would it?" Bomber asked.

"They wouldn't be able to take it off," Edith said. "There'd be no way." There was a pale vein on her temple, curving like a piece of string. "We didn't believe what you told us, you know," she said. "There was this kid, his name was Alex, and he had a boat. And he said he took this girl water-skiing he didn't like, and they were water-skiing in this little cove where swans were and he steered her right in the middle of the swans and she just creamed them, but he wasn't telling the truth. He's such a loser."

"Which one's Alex?" Bomber asked.

"Oh, he's around," Edith said.

They were silent as the passengers from the ferry eddied around them. They watched the two boys playing catch, the younger one darting from side to side, never looking backward to calculate the space, his eyes only on the softly slowly falling ball released from his brother's hand.

"That's nice, isn't it?" Edith said. "That little kid is so trusting it's kind of holy, but if his trust were misplaced it would really be holy."

Bomber wanted to touch the vein, the pimple, the shock of dark, waxed hair, but he stood motionless, slouched in his clothes. "Yeah," he said.

"Like, you know, if he fell in," Edith said.

One Sunday, May went to church. It was a denomination that, as she gratefully knew, would bury anyone. She sat in a pew behind three young women and studied their pretty blond hair, their necks and their collars and their zippers. One of the girls scratched her neck. A few minutes later, she scratched it again. May bent forward and saw a small tick crawling on the girl. She carefully picked it off with her fingers. She did it with such stealth that the girl did not even know that May had touched her. May pinched the tick vigorously between her fingernails for some time, then dropped it to the floor where it vanished from her sight.

After the service, there was a coffee hour. May joined a group around a table that was dotted with plates of muffins, bright cookies, and glazed cakes. When the conversation lagged, she said, "I've just returned from Morocco."

"How exotic!" a woman exclaimed. "Did you see the Casbah?" The group turned toward May and looked at her attentively.

"There are many Casbahs," May said. "I had tea under a tent on the edge of the Sahara. The children in Morocco all want aspirin. 'Boom-boom la tête,' they say, 'boom-boom la tête.' Their little hands are dry as paper. It's the lack of humidity, I suppose."

"You didn't go there by yourself, did you?" a fat woman asked. She was very fat and panted as she spoke.

"I went alone, yes," May said.

The group hummed appreciatively. May was holding a tiny blueberry muffin in her hand. She couldn't remember picking it up. It sat cupped in the palm of her hand, the paper around it looking like the muffin itself. May had been fooled by such muffins in public places in the past. She returned it to the table.

"I saw the blue men," May said.

The group looked at her, smiling. They were taller than she and their heads were tilted toward her.

"Most tourists don't see them," May said. "They roam the deserts. Their camels are pale beige, almost white, and the men riding them are blue. They wear deep blue floating robes and blue turbans. Their skin is even stained blue where the dye has rubbed off."

"Are they wanderers?" someone asked. "What's their purpose?"

May was startled. She felt as though the person were regarding her with suspicion.

"They're part of the mystery," she said. "To see them is to see part of the mystery."

"It must have been a sight," someone offered.

"Oh yes," May said, "it was."

After some moments, the group dispersed and May left the church and walked home through the town. May liked the town, which was cut off from other places. People came here only if they wanted to. You couldn't find this place by accident. The town seemed to be a place to visit and most people didn't stay on. There were some, of course, who had stayed on. May liked the clear light of the town and the trees rounded by the wind. She liked the trucks and the Jeeps with the dogs riding in them. When the trucks were parked, the dogs would stare solemnly down at the pavement as though there were something astounding there.

May felt elated, almost feverish. She had taken up lying rather late in life and she had taken it up with enthusiasm. Bomber didn't seem to notice, even though he had, in May's opinion, a hurtful obsession with the truth. When May got back to her house, she made herself a cup of tea and changed from her good dress into her gardening dress. She looked at herself in the mirror. I'm in charge of this person, she thought. "You'd better watch out," she said to the person in the mirror.

Bomber's friends don't drink or smoke or eat meat. They are bony and wild. In the winter, a psychiatrist comes into their classrooms and says, *You think that suicide is an escape and not a permanent departure, but the truth is it is a permanent departure.* They know that! Their eyes water with boredom. Their mothers used to lie to them when they were little about dead things, but they know better now. It's stupid to wait for the dead to do anything new. But one of their classmates had killed himself, so the psychiatrist would come back every winter.

"They planted a tree," Edith said, "you know, in this kid's memory at school and what this kid had done was hung himself from a tree." Edith rolled her eyes. "I mean this school. You're not going to believe this school."

Edith and Bomber sat on opposite sides of May's parlor, which was filling with twilight. Edith wore a pair of men's boxer shorts, lace-up boots, and a lurid Hawaiian shirt. "This is a nice house," Edith said. "It smells nice. I see your granny coming out of the Kittens sometimes. She's cute."

"A thing I used to remember about my dad," Bomber said, "was that he gave me a tepee once when I was little and he pitched it in the middle of the living room. I slept in it every night for weeks right in the middle of the living room. It was great. But it actually wasn't my dad who had done that at all, it was my gramma."

"Your granny is so cute," Edith said. "I know I'd like her. Do you know Bobby?"

"Which one's Bobby?" Bomber asked.

"He's the skinny one with the tooth that overlaps a little. He's the sort of person I used to like. What he does is he fishes. There's not a fish he can't catch."

"I can't do that," Bomber said.

"Oh, you don't have to do anything like that now," Edith said.

❧

The last things May had brought her son were a dark suit and a white shirt. They told her she could if she wished, and she

144

had. She had brought him many things in the two years before he died—candy and cigarettes and batteries, books on all subjects—and lastly she had brought these things. She had bought the shirt new and then washed it at home several times so it was soft and then she had driven over to that place. It was a cool, misty morning and the air smelled of chemicals from the mills miles away. Dew glittered on the wires and on the tips of grasses and the fronds of palms. She sat opposite him in the tall, narrow, familiar room, its high windows webby with steel, and he had opened the box with the shirt in it. Together they had looked at it. Together, mutely, they had bent their heads over it and stared. Their eyes had fallen into it as though it were a hole. They watched the shirt and it seemed to shift and shrink as though to accommodate itself to some ghastly and impossible interstice of time and purpose.

"What a shirt," her child said.

"Give it back," May whispered. She was terribly frightened. She had obliged some lunatic sense of decorum, and dread—the dread that lay beyond the fear of death—seized her.

"This is the one, I'm going out in this one," her child said. He was thin, his hair was gray.

"I wasn't thinking," May said. "Please give it back, I can't think about any of this."

"I was born to wear this shirt," her child said.

In the Lucky Kittens, over the bar, was a large painting of kittens crawling out of a sack. The sack was huge, out of proportion to the sea and the sky behind it. When May looked at it for a time, the sack appeared to tremble. One night, as she was walking home, someone brushed against her, almost knocking her down, and ran off with her purse. Her purse had fifteen dollars in it and in it too were the postcards and pictures of Morocco. May continued to walk home, her left arm still feeling the weight of the purse. It seemed heavier now that it wasn't there. She pushed herself down the street, looking, out of habit, into the lighted rooms of the handsome homes along the way. The rooms were artfully lit as though on specific display for the passerby. No one was ever seen in them. At home, she looked at herself in the mirror for bruises. There were none, although her face was deeply flushed.

"You've been robbed," she said to the face.

She went into her parlor. On the floor above, in either the gray room or the yellow room, someone shifted about. Her arm ached. She turned off the light and sat in the dark, rubbing her arm.

"The temperature of the desert can reach 175 degrees," she said aloud. "At night, it can fall below freezing. Many a time I awoke in the morning to find a sheet of ice over the water in the glass beside my bed." It was something that had been written on one of the cards. She could see it all, the writing, the words, plain as day.

Some time later, she heard Bomber's voice. "Gramma," he said, "why are you sitting in the dark?" The light was on again.

"Hi!" May said.

"Sometimes," Bomber said, "she lies out in the garden and the fog rolls in, and she stays right out there."

"The fog will be swirling around me," May said, "and Bomber will say, 'Gramma, the fog's rolled in and there you are!'" She was speaking to a figure beside Bomber with a flamboyant crest of hair. The figure was dressed in silk lounging pajamas and a pair of black work boots with steel toes.

"Gramma," Bomber said, "this is Edith."

146

"Hi!" Edith said.

"What a pretty name," May said. "There's a hybrid lily called Edith that I like very much. I'm going to plant an Edith bulb when fall comes."

"Will it come up every year?" Edith asked.

"Yes," May said.

"That is so cool," Edith said.

A few days after she had been robbed, May's purse was returned to her. It was placed in the garden, just inside the gate. Everything was there, but the bills were different. May had had a ten and a five and the new ones were singles. The cards were there. May touched one and looked at the familiar writing on the back. *It never grows dark in the desert,* the writing said. *The night sky is a deep and intense blue as though the sun were shut up behind it.* Her child had been a thoughtful tourist once, sending messages home, trying to explain things she would never see. He had never written from the prison. The thirst for explanation had left him. May thought of death. It was as though someone were bending over her, trying to blow something into her mouth. She shook her head and looked at her purse, turning it this way and that. "Where have you been?" she said to the purse. The pictures of Morocco were there. She looked through them. All there. But she didn't want them anymore. Things were never the same when they came back. She closed the purse up and dropped it in one of her large green trash cans, throwing some clipped, brown flowers over it so that it was concealed. It was less than a week later that everything was returned to her again, once more placed inside the gate. People went through the dump, she imagined, people went through the dump all the time to see what they could find. In town, the young people began calling her by name. "May," they'd say, "good morning!" They'd say, "How's it going, Gramma!" She was the condemned man's mother, and Bomber was the condemned man's son, and it didn't seem to matter what they did or didn't do, it was he who had been accepted by these people, and he who was allowing them to get by.

※

Edith was spending more and more time at May and Bomber's house. She ate dinner there several times a week. She had dyed her hair a peculiar brown color and wore scarves knotted around her neck.

"I like this look," Edith said. "It looks like I'm concealing a tracheotomy, doesn't it?"

"Your hair's good," Bomber said.

"You know what the psychiatrist at school says?" Edith said. "He says you think you want death when all you want is change."

"What is with this guy?" Bomber asked. "Is there really a problem at that place or what?"

"Oh there is, absolutely," Edith said. "You look a little like your granny. Did your dad look like her?"

"A little, I guess," Bomber said.

"You're such a bad boy," Edith said. "Such a sweet, sweet bad boy. I really love you."

The summer was over. The light had changed, and the leaves on the trees hung very still. At the Lucky Kittens, the dancing went on, but not so many people danced. When May went there, they wouldn't take her money and May submitted to this. She couldn't help herself, it seemed.

Edith helped around the house. She washed the windows with vinegar and made chocolate desserts. One evening, she said, "Do you still, like, pay income tax?"

May looked at the girl and decided to firmly lie. "No," she said.

"Well, that's good," Edith said. "It would be pretty preposterous to pay taxes after what they did."

"Of course," May said.

"But you're paying in other ways," Edith said.

"Please, dear," May said, "it was just a mistake. It doesn't mean anything in the long run," she said, dismayed at her words.

"I'll help you pay," Edith said.

With the cool weather, the tourists stopped coming. When school began, Edith asked if she could move into the yellow room. She didn't get along with her parents, she had been moving about, staying here and there with friends, but she had no real place to live, could she live in the yellow room?

May was fascinated by Edith. She did not want her in the house, above her, living in the yellow room. She felt that she and Bomber should move on, that they should try their new life together somewhere else, but she knew that this was their new life. This was the place where it appeared they had gone.

"Of course, dear," May said.

She was frightened and this surprised her, for she could scarcely believe she could know fright again after what happened to them, but there it was, some thing beyond the worst thing—some disconnection, some demand. She remembered telling Edith that she was going to plant bulbs in the garden when fall came, but she wasn't going to do it, certainly not. "No," May said to her garden, "don't even think about it." Edith moved into the yellow room. It was silent there, but May didn't listen either.

Something happened later that got around. May was driving, it was night, and the car veered off the road. Edith and Bomber were with her. The car flipped over twice, miraculously righted itself and, skidded back onto the road, the roof and fenders crushed. This was observed by a policeman who followed them for over a mile in disbelief before he pulled the car over. None of them were injured and at first they denied that anything unusual had happened at all. May said, "I thought it was just a dream, so I kept on going."

The three seemed more visible than ever after that, for they drove the car in that damaged way until winter came.

THE LAST
GENERATION

HE WAS NINE.

"Nine," his father would say, "there's an age for you. When I was nine . . ." and so on.

His father's name was Walter and he was a mechanic at a Chevrolet garage in Tallahassee. He had a seventeen-year-old brother named Walter, Jr., and he was Tommy. The boys had no mother, she had been killed in a car wreck a while before.

It had not been her fault.

The mother had taken care of houses that people rented on the river. She cleaned them and managed them for the owners. Just before she died, there had been this one house and the toilet got stopped up. I told the plumber, Tommy's mother told them, that I wanted to know just what was in that toilet because I didn't trust those tenants. I knew there was something deliberate there, not normal. I said, you tell me what you find there and when he called back he said well you wanted to know what I found there and it was fat meat and paper towels.

She had been very excited about what the plumber had told her. Tommy worried that his mother had still been thinking about this when she died—that she had been driving along, still marveling about it—fat meat and paper towels!—and that then she had been struck, and died.

She had slowed for an emergency vehicle with its lights flashing which was tearing through an intersection and a truck had crashed into her from behind. The emergency vehicle had a destination but there hadn't been an emergency at the time. It was supposed to be stationed at the stock-car races and it was late. The races—the first of the season—were just about to begin at the time of the wreck. Walter, Jr., was sitting in the old bleachers with a girl, waiting for the start, and the announcer had just called for the drivers to fire up their engines. There had been an immense roar in the sunny, dusty field, and a great cloud of insects had flown up from the rotting wood of the bleachers. The girl beside Walter, Jr., had screamed and spilled her Coke all over him. There had been thousands of the insects which were long, red, flying ants of some sort with transparent wings.

Tommy had not seen the alarming eruption of insects. He had been home, putting together a little car from a kit and painting it with silver paint.

Tommy liked rope. Sometimes he ate dirt. Fog thrilled him. He was small for his age, a weedy child. He wore blue jeans with deeply rolled cuffs for growth, although he grew slowly. Weeks often went by when he did not grow. He wore white, rather formal shirts.

The house they lived in on the river was a two-story house with a big porch, surrounded by trees. There was a panel in the ceiling which gave access to a particularly troublesome water pipe. The pipe would leak whenever it felt like it but not all the time. Apparently it had been placed by the builders at such an angle that it could neither be replaced nor repaired. Walter had placed a bucket in the crawl space between Tommy's ceiling and the floor above to catch water, and this he emptied every few weeks. Tommy believed that some living thing existed up there which needed water as all living things do, some quiet, listening, watching thing that shared his room with him. At the same time, he knew there was nothing there. Walter would throw the water from the bucket into the yard. It was important to Tommy that he always be there to see the bucket being brought down, emptied, then replaced.

In the house, with other photographs, was a photograph of Tommy and his mother taken when he was six. It had been taken on the bank of the river, the same river the rest of them still lived on, but not the same place. This place had been further upstream. Tommy was holding a fish by the tail. His mother was fat and had black hair and she was smiling at him and he was looking at the fish. He was holding the fish upside down and it was not very large but it was large enough to keep apparently. Tommy had been told that he had caught the fish and that his mother had fried it up just for him in a pan with butter and salt and that he had eaten it, but Tommy could remember none of this. What he remembered was that he had found the fish, which was not true.

Tommy loved his mother but he didn't miss her. He didn't like his father, Walter, much, and never had. He liked Walter, Jr.

Walter, Jr., had a mustache and his own Chevy truck. He liked to ride around at night with his friends and sometimes he would take Tommy on these rides. The big boys would drink beer and holler at people in Ford trucks and, in general, carry on as they tore along the river roads. Once, Tommy saw a fox and once they all saw a naked woman in a lighted window. The headlights swept past all kinds of things. One night, one of the boys pointed at a mailbox.

"See that mailbox. That's a three-hundred-dollar mailbox."

"Mailbox can't be three hundred dollars," one of the other boys screamed.

"I seen it advertised. It's totally indestructible. Door can't be pulled off. Ya hit it with a ball bat or a two-by-four, it just busts up the wood, don't hurt the box. Toss an M-80 in there, won't hurt the box."

"What's an M-80?" Tommy asked.

The big boys looked at him.

"He don't know what an M-80 is," one of them said.

Walter, Jr., stopped the truck and backed it up. They all got out and stared at the mailbox. "What kind of mail you think these people get anyway?" Walter, Jr., said.

The boys pushed at the box and peered inside. "It's just asking for it, isn't it," one of the boys said. They laughed and shrugged, and one of them pissed on it. Then they got back in the truck and drove away.

Walter, Jr., had girlfriends too. For a time, his girl was Audrey, only Audrey. Audrey had thick hair and very white, smooth skin and Tommy thought she was beautiful. Together, he thought, she and his brother were like young gods who made the world after many trials and tests, accomplishing everything only through wonders, only through self-transformations. In reality, the two were quite an ordinary couple. If anything, Audrey was peculiar looking, even ugly.

"If you marry my brother, I'll be your brother-in-law," Tommy told her.

"Ha," she said.

"Why don't you like me?" He adored her, he knew she had some power over him.

"Who wants to know?"

"Me. I want to know. Tommy."

"Who's that?" And she would laugh, twist him over, hang him upside down by the knees so he swung like a monkey, dump him on his feet again, and give him a stale stick of gum.

Then Walter, Jr., began going out with other girls.

"He dropped me," Audrey told Tommy, "just like that."

It was the end of the summer that his mother had died at the start of. Her clothes still hung in the closet. Her shoes were there too, lined up. It was the shoes that looked as though they most expected her return. Audrey came over every day and she and Tommy would sit on the porch of the house on the river in two springy steel chairs painted piggy pink. Audrey told him,

"You can't trust anybody,"

and

"Don't agree to anything."

When Walter, Jr., walked by, he never glanced at her. It was as though Audrey wasn't there. He would walk by whistling, his hair dark and crispy, his stomach flat as a board. He wore sunglasses, even though the summer had been far from bright. It had been cool and damp. The water in the river was yellow with the rains.

"Does your dad miss the Mom?" Audrey asked Tommy.

"Uh-huh."

"Who misses her the most?"

"I don't know," Tommy said. "Dad, I think."

"That's right," Audrey said. "That's what true love is. Wanting something that's missing."

She brought him presents. She gave him a big book about icebergs with colored pictures. He knew she had stolen it. They looked at the book together and Audrey read parts of it aloud.

"Icebergs were discovered by monks," Audrey said. "That's not exactly what it says here, but I'm trying to make it easier for you. Icebergs were discovered by monks who thought they were floating crystal castles." She pointed toward the river. "Squeeze your eyes up and look at the river. It looks like a cloud lying on the ground instead, see?"

He squeezed up his eyes. He could not see it.

"I like clouds," he said.

"Clouds aren't as pretty as they used to be," Audrey said. "That's a known fact."

Tommy looked back at the book. It was a big book, with nothing but pictures of icebergs or so it seemed. How could she have stolen it? She turned the pages back and forth, not turning them in any order that he could see.

"Later explorers came and discovered the sea cow," she read. "The sea cows munched seaweed in the shallows of the Bering Strait. They were colossal and dim-witted, their skin was like the bark of ancient oaks. Discovered in 1741, they were extinct by 1768."

"I don't know what extinct is," Tommy said.

"1768 was the eighteenth century. Then there was the nineteenth century and we are in the twentieth century. This is the century of destruction. The earth's been around for 4.6 billion years and it may take only fifty more years to kill it."

He thought for a while. "I'll be fifty-nine," he said. "You'll be sixty-five."

"We don't want to be around when the earth gets killed," Audrey said.

She went into the kitchen and helped herself to two popsicles from the freezer. They ate them quickly, their lips and tongues turned red.

"Do you want me to give you a kiss?" Audrey said.

He opened his mouth.

"Look," she said. "You don't drool when you kiss and you don't spit either. How'd you learn such a thing?"

"I didn't," he said.

"Never mind," she said. "We don't ever have to kiss. We're the last generation."

Walter drank more than he had when the boys' mother was alive. Still, he made them supper every night when he came home from work. He set the table, poured the milk.

"Well, men," he would say, "here we are." He would begin to cry. "I'm sorry, men," he'd say.

The sun would be setting in a mottled sky over the wet woods and the light would linger in a smeared radiance for awhile.

Tommy would scarcely be able to sleep at night, waiting for the morning to come and go so it would be the afternoon and he would be with Audrey, rocking in the metal chairs.

"The last generation has got certain responsibilities," Audrey said, "though you might think we wouldn't. We should know nothing and want nothing and be nothing, but at the same time we should want everything and know everything and be everything."

Upstairs, in his room, Walter, Jr., was lifting weights. They could hear him breathing, gasping.

Audrey's strange, smooth face looked blank. It looked empty.

"Did you love my brother?" Tommy asked. "Do you still love him?"

"Certainly not," Audrey said. "We were just passing friends."

"My father says we are all passing guests of God."

"He says that kind of thing because the Mom left so quick." She snapped her fingers.

Tommy was holding tight to the curved metal arms of the chair. He put his hands up to his face and sniffed them. He had had dreams of putting his hands in Audrey's hair, hiding them there, up to his wrists. Her hair was the color of gingerbread.

"Love isn't what you think anyway," Audrey said.

"I don't," Tommy said.

"Love is ruthless. I'm reading a book for English class, *Wuthering Heights*. Everything's in that book, but mostly it's about the ruthlessness of love."

"Tell me the whole book," Tommy said.

"Emily Brontë wrote *Wuthering Heights*. I'll tell you a story about her."

He picked at a scab on his knee.

"Emily Brontë had a bulldog named Keeper that she loved. His only bad habit was sleeping on the beds. The housekeeper complained about this and Emily said that if she ever found him sleeping on the clean white beds again, she would beat him. So Emily found him one evening sleeping on a clean white bed and she dragged him off and pushed him in a corner and beat him with her fists. She punished him until his eyes were swelled up and he was bloody and half blind, and after she punished him, she nursed him back to health."

Tommy rocked on his chair, watching Audrey. He stopped picking. The scab didn't want to come off.

"She had a harsh life," Audrey said, "but she was fair."

"Did she tell him later that she was sorry," Tommy asked.

"No. Absolutely not."

"Did Keeper forgive her?"

"Dogs aren't human. They can't forgive."

"I've never had a dog," Tommy said.

"I had a dog when I was little. She was a golden retriever. She looked exactly like all golden retrievers. Her size was the same, the color of her fur, and her large, sad eyes. Her behavior was the same. She was devoted, expectant, and yet resigned. Do you see what I mean? But I liked her a lot. She was special to me. When she died, I wanted them to bury her under my window, but you know what they said to me? They said, 'The best place to bury a dog is in your heart.' "

She looked at him until he finally said, "That's right."

"That's a crock," she said. "A crock of you know what. Don't agree to so much stuff. You've got to watch out."

"All right," he said, and shook his head.

Sometimes, Audrey visited him at school. He told her when his recess was and she would walk over to the playground and talk with him through the playground's chain-link fence. Once she brought a girlfriend with her. Her name was Flan and she wore large clothes, a long, wide skirt and a big sweater with little animals running in rows. There were only parts of the little animals where the body of the sweater met the sleeves and collar.

"Isn't he cute," Flan said. "He's like a little doll, like, isn't he."

"Now don't go and scare him," Audrey said.

Flan had a cold. She held little wadded tissues to her mouth and eyes. The tissues were blue and pink and green and she would dab at her face with them and push them back in her pockets but one spilled out and fluttered in the weeds beside the schoolyard fence. It would not blow away but stay fluttering there.

"I ain't scaring him. Where'd you get all them moles around your neck?" she said to Tommy.

"What do you mean, where'd he get them," Audrey said. "He didn't get them from anywhere."

"Don't you worry about them moles?" the girl persisted.

"Naw," Tommy said.

"You're a brave little guy, aren't you," Flan said. "There's other stuff, I know. I'm not saying it's all moles." She tugged at the front of the frightful sweater. "Audrey gave me this sweater. She stole it. You know how she steals things and after awhile she puts them back? But I like this so it's not going to get put back."

Tommy gazed unhappily at the sweater and then at Audrey.

"Sometimes putting stuff back is the best part," Audrey said. "Sometimes it isn't."

"Audrey can steal anything," Flan said.

"Can she steal a house?" Tommy asked.

"He's so *cute*," Flan shrieked.

"I gotta go in," Tommy said. Behind him, in the schoolyard, the children were playing a peculiar game. Running, crouching, calling, there didn't seem to be any rules. He trotted toward them and heard Flan say, "He's a cute little guy, isn't he."

Tommy never saw Flan again and he was glad of that. He asked Audrey if Flan was in the last generation.

"Yes," Audrey said. "She sure is."

"Is my brother in the last generation too?"

"Technically he is, of course," Audrey said. "But he's not really. He has too much stuff."

"I have stuff," Tommy said. He had his little cars. "You've given me stuff."

"But you don't have possessions because what I gave you I stole. Anyway, you'll stop caring about that soon. You'll forget all about it but Walter, Jr., really likes possessions and he likes to think about what he's going to do. He has his truck and his barbells and those shirts with the pearl buttons."

"He wants a pair of lizard boots for his birthday," Tommy said.

"Isn't that pathetic," Audrey said.

Every night, Walter would come home from work, scrub down his hands and arms, set the table, pour the milk. The boys sat on either side of him. The chair where their mother used to sit looked out at the yard, at a woodpile there.

"Men," Walter began, "when I was your age, I didn't know . . ." He shook his head and drank his whiskey, his eyes filling with tears.

He had been forgetting to empty the bucket in the space above Tommy's room. A pale stain had spread upon the ceiling. Tommy showed it to Audrey.

"That's nice," she said, "the shape, all dappled brown and yellow like that, but it doesn't tell you anything really. It's just part of the doomed reality all around us." She climbed up and brought the bucket down.

"A monk would take this water and walk into the desert and pour it over a dry and broken stick there," she said. "That's why people become monks, because they get sick of being around doomed reality all the time."

"Let's be monks," he said.

161

"Monks love solitude," Audrey said. "They love solitude more than anything. When monks started out, long, long ago, they were waiting for the end of time."

"But the end of time didn't happen, did it?" Tommy asked.

"It was too soon then. They didn't know what we know today."

She wore silver sandals. Once she had broken a strap on the sandal and Tommy had fixed it with his Hot Stuff Instant Glue.

"Someday we could have a little boy just like you," she said, "And we'd call him Tommy Two."

But he was not fond of this idea. He was afraid that it would come out of him somehow, this Tommy Two, that he would make it and be ashamed. So, together, they dismissed the notion.

One day, Walter, Jr., said to him, "Look, Audrey shouldn't be hanging around here all the time. She's weird. She's no mommy, believe me."

"I don't need a mommy," Tommy said.

"She's mad at me and she's trying to get back at me through you. She's just practicing on you. You don't want to be practiced on, do you? She's just a very unhappy person."

"I'm unhappy," Tommy said.

"You need to get out and play some games. Soccer, maybe."

"Why?" Tommy said. "I don't like Daddy."

"You're just trying that out," Walter, Jr., said. "You like him well enough."

"Audrey and me are the last generation and you're not," Tommy said.

"What are you talking about?"

"You should be but you're not. Nothing can be done about it."

"Let's drive around in the truck," Walter, Jr., said.

Tommy still enjoyed riding around in the truck. They passed by the houses their mother had cleaned. They looked all right. Someone else was cleaning them now.

"You don't look good," Walter, Jr., said. "You're too pale. You mope around all the time."

Inside the truck, the needle of the black compass on the dashboard trembled. The compass box was filled with what seemed like water. Maybe it was water. Tommy was looking at everything carefully, but trying not to think about it. Audrey was teaching him how to do this. He remembered at some point to turn toward his brother and smile, and this made his brother feel better, it was clear.

The winter nights were cool. Audrey and Tommy still sat in their chairs at dusk on the porch but now they wrapped themselves in blankets.

"Walter, Jr., is dating a lot anymore," Audrey said. "It's nice we have these evenings to ourselves but we should take little trips, you know? I have a lot to show you. Have you ever been to the TV tower north of town?"

The father, Walter, was already in bed. He worked and drank and slept. He had saved the fragments of soap his wife had left behind in the shower. He had wrapped them in tissue paper and placed them in a drawer. But he was sleeping in the middle of the bed these nights, hardly aware of it.

"No," Tommy said. "Is it in the woods?"

"It's a lot taller than the woods and it's not far away from here. It's called Tall Timbers. It's right smack in the middle of birds' migration routes. Thousands of birds run into it every year, all kinds of them. We can go out there and look at the birds."

Tommy was puzzled. "Are the birds dead?"

"Yes," she said. "In an eleven-year period, thirty thousand birds of a hundred and seventy species have been found at the base of the tower."

"Why don't they move it?"

"They don't do things like that," Audrey said. "It would never occur to them."

He did not want to see the birds around the tower. "Let's go," he said.

"We'll go in the spring. That's when the birds change latitudes. That's when they move from one place to another. There's a little tiny warbler bird that used to live around here in the spring, but people haven't seen it for years. They haven't found it at the base of any of the TV towers. They used to find it there, that's how they knew it wasn't extinct."

"Monks used to live on top of tall towers," Tommy said, for she had told him this. "If a monk stayed up there, he could keep the birds away, he could wave his arms around or something so they wouldn't hit."

"Monks live in a cool, crystalline half-darkness of the mind and heart," Audrey said. "They couldn't be bothered with that."

They rocked in their chairs on the porch. The porch had been painted a succession of colors. Where the chairs had scraped the wood there was light green, dark green, blue, red. Bugs crawled around the lights.

"If I got sick, would you stay with me?" Tommy asked.

"I'm not sure. It would depend."

"My mommy would have stayed."

"Well you never know," Audrey said. "You got to realize

mommies get tired. They're willing to let things go sometimes. They get to thinking and they're off."

"Do you have a mommy?" he asked cautiously.

"Technically I do," Audrey said, "but she's gone as your mommy actually. Before something's gone, it had to have been there right? Even so, I don't feel any rancor about her. It's important not to feel rancor."

"I don't feel rancor," Tommy said.

Then one afternoon, Walter came home from his work at the garage and it was as though he had woken from a strange sleep. He didn't appear startled by his awakening. His days and nights of grief came to an end really with no harder shock than that of a boat's keel grounding upon a river's shore. He stopped drinking and weeping. He put his wife's things in cardboard boxes and stored the boxes. In fact, he stored them in the space above Tommy's room.

"Why's that girl here all the time?" Walter asked. "She's not still Walter, Jr.'s girlfriend, is she?"

He said, "She shouldn't be here all the time."

"Audrey's my friend," Tommy said.

"She's not a nice girl. She's too old to be your friend."

"Then I'm too young to be your friend."

"No, honey, you're my son."

"I don't like you," Tommy said.

"You love me but you don't like me, is that it?" Walter was thinner and cleaner. He spoke cheerfully.

Tommy considered this. He shook his head.

At school, at the edge of the playground, Audrey talked through the chain-link fence to Tommy.

"You know that pretty swamp close by? It's full of fish, all different kinds. You know how they know?"

He didn't.

"They poison little patches of it. They put out nets and then they drop the poison in. It settles in the gills of the fish and suffocates them. The fish pop up to the surface and then they drag them out and classify and weigh and measure each one."

"Who?" Tommy said.

"They do it a couple times a year to see if there's as many different kinds and as many as before. That's how they count things. That's their attitude. They act as though they care about stuff, but they don't. They're just pretending."

Tommy told her that his father didn't want her to come over to the house, that he wasn't supposed to talk to her any more.

"The Dad's back is he," Audrey said. "What it is is that he thinks he can start over. That's pathetic."

"What are we going to do?" Tommy said.

"You shouldn't listen to him," Audrey said. "Why are you listening to him? We're the last generation, there's something else we're listening to."

They were silent for awhile, listening. The other children had gone inside.

"What is it?" Tommy asked.

"You'll recognize it when you hear it. Something will happen, something unusual for which we were always prepared. The Dad's life has already taken a turn for the worse, it's obvious. It's like he's a stranger now, walking down the wrong road. Do you see what I mean? I could put it another way."

"Put it another way," Tommy said.

"It's his life that's like the stranger, standing real still. A stranger standing alongside a dark road, waiting for him to pass."

It appeared his father was able to keep Audrey away. Tommy wouldn't have thought it was possible. He knew his father was powerless, but Audrey wasn't coming around. His father moved through the house in his dark, oiled boots, fixing things. He painted the kitchen, restacked the woodpile. He replaced the pipe above the ceiling in Tommy's room. It had long been accepted that this could not be done, but now it was done, it did not leak, there was no need for the bucket. The bucket was used now to take ashes from the woodstove. Walter, Jr., had a job in the gym he worked out in. He had long, hard muscles, a distracted air. He worried about girls, about money. He wanted an apartment of his own, in town.

Tommy lived alone with his father. "Talk to me, son," Walter said. "I love you."

Tommy said nothing. His father disgusted him a little. He was like a tree walking, strange but not believable. He was trying to start over. It was pathetic.

Tommy only saw Audrey on schooldays, at recess. He waited by the fence for her in the vitreous, intractable light of the southern afternoon.

"I had a boy tell me once my nipples were like bowls of Wheaties," Audrey said.

"When," Tommy said. "No."

"That's a simile. Similes are a crock. There's no more time for similes. There used to be that kind of time, but no more. You shouldn't see what you're seeing thinking it looks like something else. They haven't left us with much but the things that are left should be seen as they are."

Some days she did not come by. Then he would see her waiting at the fence, or she would appear suddenly, while he was waiting there. But then days passed, more days than there had been before. Days with Walter saying,

"We need each other, son. We're not over this yet. We have to help each other. I need your help."

It was suppertime. They were sitting at a table over the last of a meal Walter had put together.

"I want Audrey back," Tommy said.

"Audrey?" Walter looked surprised. "Walter, Jr., heard about what happened to Audrey. She made her bed as they say, now she's got to lie in it." He looked at Tommy, then dismayed, looked away.

"Who wants you," Tommy said. "Nobody."

Walter rubbed his head with his hands. He looked around the room, at some milk on the floor that Tommy had spilled. The house was empty except for them. There were no animals around, nothing. It was all beyond what was possible, he knew.

In the night, Tommy heard his father moving around, bumping into things, moaning. A glass fell. He heard it breaking for what seemed a long time. The air in the house felt close, sour. He pushed open his bedroom window and felt the air fluttering warmly against his skin. Down along the river, the water popped and smacked against the muddy bank. It was close to the season when he and Audrey could go to the tower where all the birds were. He could feel it in the air. Audrey would come for him from wherever she was, from wherever they had made her go, and they would go to the tower and find the little warbler bird. Then they would know that it still existed because they had found it dead there. He and Audrey would be the ones who would find it. They were the last generation, the ones who would see everything for the last time. That's what the last generation does.